I0596039

"Sure the fight was fixed. I fixed it with
a right hand" - *George Foreman*

THE CLINCH

THE CLINCH

The Pugilism Anthology

JACK LONDON

Introduction copyright © 2020 by J. Lawrence Mitchell.

Printed in the United States of America. All rights reserved under International and Pan-American Copyright Conventions. Published in the United States by Circle Up Stories LLC, 522 Crafton Ave., Pitman, NJ 08071.

The "Circle Up Stories" logo is the exclusive property of Circle Up Stories LLC. Circle Up Stories is an imprint of Circle Up Stories LLC.

Text set in PT Serif and Playfair Display. Cover photo by Skitterphoto from Pexels with additional illustration by PipandJ Papery.

Library of Congress Control Number: 2019956408

ISBN (paperback): 978-1-7343702-0-1

ISBN (ebook): 978-1-7343702-1-8

www.circleupstories.com

Contents

INTRODUCTION

BORN IN SAN FRANCISCO, though reared primarily in a rough section of Oakland, Jack London (1876-1916) knew hard times as a child but was a fighter all his life. He was an illegitimate child in an unstable family that suffered repeated misfortune despite the efforts of his proud, if distant, mother and his kindly stepfather. A failed farming experiment in the Livermore Valley followed a failed grocery store and Jack was thus a member of "a tumbleweed family, blowing with the winds of failure," as Andrew Sinclair put it (Sinclair, 6).

Unsurprisingly, he was something of a delinquent in school and out, restless and all-too-often embroiled in fights with neighborhood boys. His boyhood friend, Frank Atherton, describes one memorable fight with Mike Panella, leader of the "Cole [Grammar School] hoodlums" in which Jack showed his mettle and triumphed, albeit with bloody knuckles (Kingman, 32). And yet, by the age of ten, he had also found escape from the desolation of daily life in books, frequenting the public library and becoming "an omnivorous reader" (Letters, 148) and, in time, an autodidact.

In maturity, London emerged as a driven-but-disciplined, writer whose many real-life adventures as oyster pirate, sailor and seal-hunter, hobo and witness to the Klondike gold rush were transmuted into memorable and still widely admired novels and stories. He also came to appreciate the value of physical fitness and to take pride in his own physique, remembering ruefully a couple of years before his death: "I once, in the long ago, had a beautiful body, and was proud as the devil of it" (letter to Edward DeWitt, 23 September 1914).

Whatever his experience as a rough-house fighter in his youth on the Oakland wharfs—and our knowledge thereof derives, for the most part, from his own fictionalized accounts—London really knew nothing of boxing as such until he joined the Socialist Labor Party in Oakland in 1896 where he met and formed a warm friendship with Herman 'Jim' Whitaker. A former certified physical fitness instructor in the British Army some ten years older than London, Whitaker shared London's commitment to writing and politics, and "taught Jack the fine points of boxing and fencing" (Kingman, 93). The lessons with Whitaker no doubt helped eliminate the sort of crude roundhouse swings predominant on the wharfs and laid the foundation for a life-long proclivity for impromptu sparring sessions with friends and acquaintances, above all with his soul-mate and spouse, Charmian. Sparring provided a good workout, of course; but it also reinforced London's self-image as "a rough savage fellow... who likes prizefights and brutalities" (letter to Charmain Kittredge, 18 June 1903).

Inevitably, his enthusiasm for such affairs is reflected in his wide-ranging fiction in which boxing references and allusions are not uncommon, if sometimes unacknowledged: Billy Roberts, the protagonist of The Valley of the Moon (1913) is a professional boxer and a teamster; and one story in The Strength of the Strong (1914) features the heavyweight champion of the Navy, "a big brute of a man, a veritable gorilla." But it is on the strength of two novellas, *The Game* (1905) and *The Abysmal Brute* (1913) and two stories, "A Piece of Steak" (1909) and "The Mexican" (1911) that London merits recognition as a pioneer boxing writer.

To some extent, London's boxing stories draw upon his boxing journalism. His first sporting article, "Gladiators of Machine Age," for Hearst's *San Francisco Examiner*, was a next-day account of the Jeffries-Ruhlin heavyweight championship fight of 15 November 1901, in truth a rather one-sided affair from which Ruhlin withdrew after the fifth round. London represented the champion, Jim Jeffries, in atavistic terms as "a big dark male, hairy of chest and body" and thus, in effect, bound to win: "it was patent that one was a fighter, that the other was not". There was more than a little poetic license in London's contrast between the two fighters—Ruhlin, "the Akron Giant," was at least as dark in coloring, if not as hairy-chested as his opponent. A few years after this report, echoes of this descriptive language make their way into *The Game*: one fighter is described as "primordial, ferocious... covered with a hairy growth that matted like a dog's on his chest and shoulders."

London also reported on the historic second bout of 5 September 1905 between lightweight champion Jimmy Britt and Oscar "Battling" Nelson, often dubbed "the Durable Dane." In recording Nelson's somewhat unexpected victory, London wrote, "It was the abysmal brute [Nelson] against a more highly organized, intelligent creature [Britt]." Understandably, Nelson didn't appreciate this characterization and said so. London responded that it was intended as a compliment and explained that Nelson had "to an unusual degree the brute that you and I and all of us possess in varying degrees", whereas Britt was "too far removed from the brute" (*Life, Battles and Career of Battling Nelson*, 178-79).

This notion of an underlying primordial or atavistic element was already a well-developed part of London's worldview and can be traced through many of his works. In *White Fang* (1906) the once-domesticated White Fang becomes the "dominant primordial beast" by killing Spitz, the lead dog of the dogsled team, largely as a result of his treatment by Beauty Smith, the sadistic owner, in whom "the abysmal brute had been rising". This key concept would crop up again in *Before Adam* (1907), *The Iron Heel* (1908), and *Martin Eden* (1909) before ultimately surfacing as title and topic in *The Abysmal Brute* (1913).

It is worth noting that on 27 June 1910 in the *New York Herald*, as part of his coverage for the upcoming World Heavyweight championship between Jack Johnson and former title holder Jim Jeffries in July of that same year, London concluded that the "fighter with the quality of the

'Abysmal Brute' will win the great battle." But the hairy-chested Jeffries, the "Great White Hope," was no match for the consummate defensive boxer, Johnson, and London would have to recalibrate his conception of the term in his novella published three years later.

J. Lawrence Mitchell
Professor Emeritus, Department of English
Texas A&M University, College Station, TX

Deeper Reading and References:

Bankes, James, ed. *Jack London: Stories of Boxing.* 1992. William C. Brown, Dubuque, IA.

Hendricks, K., Earl Labor and Irving Shephard, eds. *The Letters of Jack London.* 1988. Stanford University Press, Stanford, CA.

Kingman, Russ. *A Pictorial Biography of Jack London.* 1979. Jack London Research Center. Glen Ellen, CA.

London, Jack. "Gladiators of Machine Age," *San Francisco Examiner,* 16 November 1909, 1-2.

London, Jack. "How Different People View Fighters: Brain Beaten by Brute Force," *Life, Battles and Career of Battling Nelson.* 1909. Hegewisch, IL.

Mitchell, J. Lawrence. "Jack London and Boxing," *American Literary Realism,* Spring 2004, Vol. 36, No. 3, 225-242.

Sinclair, Andrew. *Jack: A Biography of Jack London.* 1977. Harper and Row, New York, NY.

Williams, Jay ed. *The Oxford Handbook of Jack London.* 2017. Oxford University Press. Oxford.

THE GAME

CHAPTER 1

MANY PATTERNS OF CARPET lay rolled out before them on the floor—two of Brussels showed the beginning of their quest, and its ending in that direction; while a score of ingrains lured their eyes and prolonged the debate between desire pocket-book. The head of the department did them the honor of waiting upon them himself—or did Joe the honor, as she well knew, for she had noted the open-mouthed awe of the elevator boy who brought them up. Nor had she been blind to the marked respect shown Joe by the urchins and groups of young fellows on corners, when she walked with him in their own neighborhood down at the west end of the town.

But the head of the department was called away to the telephone, and in her mind the splendid promise of the carpets and the irk of the pocket-book were thrust aside by a greater doubt and anxiety.

"But I don't see what you find to like in it, Joe," she said softly, the note of insistence in her words betraying recent and unsatisfactory discussion.

For a fleeting moment a shadow darkened his boyish face, to be replaced by the glow of tenderness. He was only a boy, as she was only a girl—two young things on the threshold of life, house-renting and buying carpets together.

"What's the good of worrying?" he questioned. "It's the last go, the very last."

He smiled at her, but she saw on his lips the unconscious and all but breathed sigh of renunciation, and with the instinctive monopoly of woman for her mate, she feared this thing she did not understand and which gripped his life so strongly.

"You know the go with O'Neil cleared the last payment on mother's house," he went on. "And that's off my mind. Now this last with Ponta will give me a hundred dollars in bank—an even hundred, that's the purse—for you and me to start on, a nest-egg."

She disregarded the money appeal. "But you like it, this—this 'game' you call it. Why?"

He lacked speech-expression. He expressed himself with his hands, at his work, and with his body and the play of his muscles in the squared ring; but to tell with his own lips the charm of the squared ring was beyond him. Yet he essayed, and haltingly at first, to express what he felt and analyzed when playing the Game at the supreme summit of existence.

"All I know, Genevieve, is that you feel good in the ring when you've got the man where you want him, when he's had a punch up both sleeves waiting for you and you've never given him an opening to land 'em, when you've landed your own little punch an' he's goin' groggy, an' holdin' on, an' the referee's dragging him off so's you can go in an' finish 'm, an' all the house is shouting an' tearin' itself loose, an' you know you're the best man, an' that you played m' fair an' won out because you're the best man. I tell you—"

He ceased brokenly, alarmed by his own volubility and by Genevieve's look of alarm. As he talked she had watched his face while fear dawned in her own. As he described the moment of moments to her, on his inward vision were lined the tottering man, the lights, the shouting house, and he swept out and away from her on this tide of life that was beyond her comprehension, menacing, irresistible, making her love pitiful and weak. The Joe she knew receded, faded, became lost. The fresh boyish face was gone, the tenderness of the eyes, the sweetness of the mouth with its curves and pictured corners. It was a man's face she saw, a face of steel, tense and immobile; a mouth of steel, the lips like the jaws of a trap; eyes of steel, dilated, intent, and the light in them and the glitter were the light and glitter of steel. The face of a man, and she had known only his boy face. This face she did not know at all.

And yet, while it frightened her, she was vaguely stirred with pride in him. His masculinity, the masculinity of the fighting male, made its inevitable appeal to her, a female, moulded by all her heredity to seek out the strong man for mate, and to lean against the wall of his strength. She did not understand this force of his being that rose mightier than her love and laid its compulsion upon him; and yet, in her woman's heart she was aware of the sweet pang which told her that for her sake, for Love's own sake, he had surrendered to her, abandoned all that portion of his life, and with this one last fight would never fight again.

"Mrs. Silverstein doesn't like prize-fighting," she said. "She's down on it, and she knows something, too."

He smiled indulgently, concealing a hurt, not altogether new, at her persistent inappreciation of this side of his nature and life in which he took the greatest pride. It was to him power and achievement, earned by his own effort and hard work; and in the moment when he had offered himself and all that he was to Genevieve, it was this, and this alone, that he was proudly conscious of laying at her feet. It was the merit of work performed, a guerdon of manhood finer and greater than any other man could offer, and it had been to him his justification and right to possess her. And she had not understood it then, as she did not understand it now, and he might well have wondered what else she found in him to make him worthy.

"Mrs. Silverstein is a dub, and a softy, and a knocker," he said good-humoredly. "What's she know about such things, anyway? I tell you it is good, and healthy, too,"—this last as an afterthought. "Look at me. I tell you I have to live clean to be in condition like this. I live cleaner than she does, or her old man, or anybody you know—baths, rub-downs, exercise, regular hours, good food and no makin' a pig of myself, no drinking, no smoking, nothing that'll hurt me. Why, I live cleaner than you, Genevieve—"

"Honest, I do," he hastened to add at sight of her shocked face. "I don't mean water an' soap, but look there." His hand closed reverently but firmly on her arm. "Soft, you're all soft, all over. Not like mine. Here, feel this."

He pressed the ends of her fingers into his hard

arm-muscles until she winced from the hurt.

"Hard all over just like that," he went on. "Now that's what I call clean. Every bit of flesh an' blood an' muscle is clean right down to the bones—and they're clean, too. No soap and water only on the skin, but clean all the way in. I tell you it feels clean. It knows it's clean itself. When I wake up in the morning an' go to work, every drop of blood and bit of meat is shouting right out that it is clean. Oh, I tell you—"

He paused with swift awkwardness, again confounded by his unwonted flow of speech. Never in his life had he been stirred to such utterance, and never in his life had there been cause to be so stirred. For it was the Game that had been questioned, its verity and worth, the Game itself, the biggest thing in the world—or what had been the biggest thing in the world until that chance afternoon and that chance purchase in Silverstein's candy store, when Genevieve loomed suddenly colossal in his life, overshadowing all other things. He was beginning to see, though vaguely, the sharp conflict between woman and career, between a man's work in the world and woman's need of the man. But he was not capable of generalization. He saw only the antagonism between the concrete, flesh-and-blood Genevieve and the great, abstract, living Game. Each resented the other, each claimed him; he was torn with the strife, and yet drifted helpless on the currents of their contention.

His words had drawn Genevieve's gaze to his face, and she had pleasured in the clear skin, the clear eyes, the cheek soft and smooth as a girl's. She saw the force of his argument and disliked it accordingly. She revolted instinctively against this Game which drew him away from her, robbed her of part of him. It was a rival she did not understand. Nor could she understand its seductions. Had it been a woman rival, another girl, knowledge and light and sight would have been hers. As it was, she grappled in the dark with an intangible adversary about which she knew nothing. What truth she felt in his speech made the Game but the more formidable.

A sudden conception of her weakness came to her. She felt pity for herself, and sorrow. She wanted him, all of him, her woman's need would not be satisfied with less; and he eluded her, slipped away here and there from the embrace with which she tried to clasp him. Tears swam into her eyes, and her lips trembled, turning defeat into victory, routing the all-potent Game with the strength of her weakness.

"Don't, Genevieve, don't," the boy pleaded, all contrition, though he was confused and dazed. To his masculine mind there was nothing relevant about her breakdown; yet all else was forgotten at sight of her tears.

She smiled forgiveness through her wet eyes, and though he knew of nothing for which to be forgiven, he melted utterly. His hand went out impulsively to hers, but she avoided the clasp by a sort of bodily stiffening and chill, the while the eyes smiled still more gloriously.

"Here comes Mr. Clausen," she said, at the same time, by some transforming alchemy of woman, presenting to the newcomer eyes that showed no hint of moistness.

"Think I was never coming back, Joe?" queried the

head of the department, a pink-and-white-faced man, whose austere side-whiskers were belied by genial little eyes.

"Now let me see—hum, yes, we was discussing ingrains," he continued briskly. "That tasty little pattern there catches your eye, don't it now, eh? Yes, yes, I know all about it. I set up housekeeping when I was getting fourteen a week. But nothing's too good for the little nest, eh? Of course I know, and it's only seven cents more, and the dearest is the cheapest, I say. Tell you what I'll do, Joe,"—this with a burst of philanthropic impulsiveness and a confidential lowering of voice,—"seein's it's you, and I wouldn't do it for anybody else, I'll reduce it to five cents. Only,"—here his voice became impressively solemn,—"only you mustn't ever tell how much you really did pay."

"Sewed, lined, and laid—of course that's included," he said, after Joe and Genevieve had conferred together and announced their decision.

"And the little nest, eh?" he queried. "When do you spread your wings and fly away? To-morrow! So soon? Beautiful! Beautiful!"

He rolled his eyes ecstatically for a moment, then beamed upon them with a fatherly air.

Joe had replied sturdily enough, and Genevieve had blushed prettily; but both felt that it was not exactly proper. Not alone because of the privacy and holiness of the subject, but because of what might have been prudery in the middle class, but which in them was the modesty and reticence found in individuals of the working class when they strive after clean living and morality.

Mr. Clausen accompanied them to the elevator, all

smiles, patronage, and beneficence, while the clerks turned their heads to follow Joe's retreating figure.

"And to-night, Joe?" Mr. Clausen asked anxiously, as they waited at the shaft. "How do you feel? Think you'll do him?"

"Sure," Joe answered. "Never felt better in my life."

"You feel all right, eh? Good! Good! You see, I was just a-wonderin'—you know, ha! ha!—goin' to get married and the rest—thought you might be unstrung, eh, a trifle?—nerves just a bit off, you know. Know how gettin' married is myself. But you're all right, eh? Of course you are. No use asking you that. Ha! ha! Well, good luck, my boy! I know you'll win. Never had the least doubt, of course, of course."

"And good-by, Miss Pritchard," he said to Genevieve, gallantly handing her into the elevator. "Hope you call often. Will be charmed—charmed—I assure you."

"Everybody calls you 'Joe'," she said reproachfully, as the car dropped downward. "Why don't they call you 'Mr. Fleming'? That's no more than proper."

But he was staring moodily at the elevator boy and did not seem to hear.

"What's the matter, Joe?" she asked, with a tenderness the power of which to thrill him she knew full well.

"Oh, nothing," he said. "I was only thinking—and wishing."

"Wishing?—what?" Her voice was seduction itself, and her eyes would have melted stronger than he, though they failed in calling his up to them.

Then, deliberately, his eyes lifted to hers. "I was wishing you could see me fight just once."

She made a gesture of disgust, and his face fell. It came to her sharply that the rival had thrust between and was bearing him away.

"I—I'd like to," she said hastily with an effort, striving after that sympathy which weakens the strongest men and draws their heads to women's breasts.

"Will you?"

Again his eyes lifted and looked into hers. He meant it—she knew that. It seemed a challenge to the greatness of her love.

"It would be the proudest moment of my life," he said simply.

It may have been the apprehensiveness of love, the wish to meet his need for her sympathy, and the desire to see the Game face to face for wisdom's sake,—and it may have been the clarion call of adventure ringing through the narrow confines of uneventful existence; for a great daring thrilled through her, and she said, just as simply, "I will."

"I didn't think you would, or I wouldn't have asked," he confessed, as they walked out to the sidewalk.

"But can't it be done?" she asked anxiously, before her resolution could cool.

"Oh, I can fix that; but I didn't think you would."

"I didn't think you would," he repeated, still amazed, as he helped her upon the electric car and felt in his pocket for the fare.

CHAPTER 2

GENEVIEVE AND JOE were working-class aristocrats. In an environment made up largely of sordidness and wretchedness they had kept themselves unsullied and wholesome. Theirs was a self-respect, a regard for the niceties and clean things of life, which had held them aloof from their kind. Friends did not come to them easily; nor had either ever possessed a really intimate friend, a heart-companion with whom to chum and have things in common. The social instinct was strong in them, yet they had remained lonely because they could not satisfy that instinct and at that same time satisfy their desire for cleanness and decency.

If ever a girl of the working class had led the sheltered life, it was Genevieve. In the midst of roughness and brutality, she had shunned all that was rough and brutal. She saw but what she chose to see, and she chose always to see the best, avoiding coarseness and uncouthness without effort, as a matter of instinct. To begin with, she had been peculiarly unexposed. An only child, with an invalid mother upon whom she attended, she had not joined in the street games and frolics of the children of the neighbourhood. Her father, a mild-tempered, narrow-chested, anæmic little clerk, domestic because of his inherent disability to mix with men, had done his full share toward giving the home an atmosphere of sweetness and tenderness.

An orphan at twelve, Genevieve had gone straight from her father's funeral to live with the Silversteins in their rooms above the candy store; and here, sheltered by kindly aliens, she earned her keep and clothes by waiting on the shop. Being Gentile, she was especially necessary to the Silversteins, who would not run the business themselves when the day of their Sabbath came round.

And here, in the uneventful little shop, six maturing years had slipped by. Her acquaintances were few. She had elected to have no girl chum for the reason that no satisfactory girl had appeared. Nor did she choose to walk with the young fellows of the neighbourhood, as was the custom of girls from their fifteenth year. "That stuck-up doll-face," was the way the girls of the neighbourhood described her; and though she earned their enmity by her beauty and aloofness, she none the less commanded their respect. "Peaches and cream," she was called by the young men—though softly and amongst themselves, for they were afraid of arousing the ire of the other girls, while they stood in awe of Genevieve, in a dimly religious way, as a something mysteriously beautiful and unapproachable.

For she was indeed beautiful. Springing from a long

line of American descent, she was one of those wonderful working-class blooms which occasionally appear, defying all precedent of forebears and environment, apparently without cause or explanation. She was a beauty in color, the blood spraying her white skin so deliciously as to earn for her the apt description, "peaches and cream." She was a beauty in the regularity of her features; and, if for no other reason, she was a beauty in the mere delicacy of the lines on which she was moulded. Quiet, low-voiced, stately, and dignified, she somehow had the knack of dress, and but befitted her beauty and dignity with anything she put on. Withal, she was sheerly feminine, tender and soft and clinging, with the smouldering passion of the mate and the motherliness of the woman. But this side of her nature had lain dormant through the years, waiting for the mate to appear.

Then Joe came into Silverstein's shop one hot Saturday afternoon to cool himself with ice-cream soda. She had not noticed his entrance, being busy with one other customer, an urchin of six or seven who gravely analyzed his desires before the show-case wherein truly generous and marvellous candy creations reposed under a cardboard announcement, "Five for Five Cents."

She had heard, "Ice-cream soda, please," and had herself asked, "What flavor?" without seeing his face. For that matter, it was not a custom of hers to notice young men. There was something about them she did not understand. The way they looked at her made her uncomfortable, she knew not why; while there was an uncouthness and roughness about them that did not please her. As yet, her imagination had been untouched by man.

The young fellows she had seen had held no lure for her, had been without meaning to her. In short, had she been asked to give one reason for the existence of men on the earth, she would have been nonplussed for a reply.

As she emptied the measure of ice-cream into the glass, her casual glance rested on Joe's face, and she experienced on the instant a pleasant feeling of satisfaction. The next instant his eyes were upon her face, her eyes had dropped, and she was turning away toward the soda fountain. But at the fountain, filling the glass, she was impelled to look at him again—but for no more than an instant, for this time she found his eyes already upon her, waiting to meet hers, while on his face was a frankness of interest that caused her quickly to look away.

That such pleasingness would reside for her in any man astonished her. "What a pretty boy," she thought to herself, innocently and instinctively trying to ward off the power to hold and draw her that lay behind the mere prettiness. "Besides, he isn't pretty," she thought, as she placed the glass before him, received the silver dime in payment, and for the third time looked into his eyes. Her vocabulary was limited, and she knew little of the worth of words; but the strong masculinity of his boy's face told her that the term was inappropriate.

"He must be handsome, then," was her next thought, as she again dropped her eyes before his. But all good-looking men were called handsome, and that term, too, displeased her. But whatever it was, he was good to see, and she was irritably aware of a desire to look at him again and again.

As for Joe, he had never seen anything like this girl across the counter. While he was wiser in natural philosophy than she, and could have given immediately the reason for woman's existence on the earth, nevertheless woman had no part in his cosmos. His imagination was as untouched by woman as the girl's was by man. But his imagination was touched now, and the woman was Genevieve. He had never dreamed a girl could be so beautiful, and he could not keep his eyes from her face. Yet every time he looked at her, and her eyes met his, he felt painful embarrassment, and would have looked away had not her eyes dropped so quickly.

But when, at last, she slowly lifted her eyes and held their gaze steadily, it was his own eyes that dropped, his own cheek that mantled red. She was much less embarrassed than he, while she betrayed her embarrassment not at all. She was aware of a flutter within, such as she had never known before, but in no way did it disturb her outward serenity. Joe, on the contrary, was obviously awkward and delightfully miserable.

Neither knew love, and all that either was aware was an overwhelming desire to look at the other. Both had been troubled and roused, and they were drawing together with the sharpness and imperativeness of uniting elements. He toyed with his spoon, and flushed his embarrassment over his soda, but lingered on; and she spoke softly, dropped her eyes, and wove her witchery about him.

But he could not linger forever over a glass of ice-cream soda, while he did not dare ask for a second glass. So he left her to remain in the shop in a waking trance, and went away himself down the street like a somnambulist.

Genevieve dreamed through the afternoon and knew that she was in love. Not so with Joe. He knew only that he wanted to look at her again, to see her face. His thoughts did not get beyond this, and besides, it was scarcely a thought, being more a dim and inarticulate desire.

The urge of this desire he could not escape. Day after day it worried him, and the candy shop and the girl behind the counter continually obtruded themselves. He fought off the desire. He was afraid and ashamed to go back to the candy shop. He solaced his fear with, "I ain't a ladies' man." Not once, nor twice, but scores of times, he muttered the thought to himself, but it did no good. And by the middle of the week, in the evening, after work, he came into the shop. He tried to come in carelessly and casually, but his whole carriage advertised the strong effort of will that compelled his legs to carry his reluctant body thither. Also, he was shy, and awkwarder than ever. Genevieve, on the contrary, was serener than ever, though fluttering most alarmingly within. He was incapable of speech, mumbled his order, looked anxiously at the clock, despatched his ice-cream soda in tremendous haste, and was gone.

She was ready to weep with vexation. Such meagre reward for four days' waiting, and assuming all the time that she loved! He was a nice boy and all that, she knew, but he needn't have been in so disgraceful a hurry. But Joe had not reached the corner before he wanted to be back with her again. He just wanted to look at her. He had no thought that it was love. Love? That was when young fellows and girls walked out together. As for him—And then his desire took sharper shape, and he discovered that that was the very thing he wanted her to do. He wanted to see her, to look at her, and well could he do all this if she but walked out with him. Then that was why the young fellows and girls walked out together, he mused, as the week-end drew near. He had remotely considered this walking out to be a mere form or observance preliminary to matrimony. Now he saw the deeper wisdom in it, wanted it himself, and concluded therefrom that he was in love.

Both were now of the same mind, and there could be but the one ending; and it was the mild nine days' wonder of Genevieve's neighborhood when she and Joe walked out together.

Both were blessed with an avarice of speech, and because of it their courtship was a long one. As he expressed himself in action, she expressed herself in repose and control, and by the love-light in her eyes—though this latter she would have suppressed in all maiden modesty had she been conscious of the speech her heart printed so plainly there. "Dear" and "darling" were too terribly intimate for them to achieve quickly; and, unlike most mating couples, they did not overwork the love-words. For a long time they were content to walk together in the evenings, or to sit side by side on a bench in the park, neither uttering a word for an hour at a time, merely gazing into each other's eyes, too faintly luminous in the starshine to be a cause for self-consciousness and embarrassment.

He was as chivalrous and delicate in his attention as any knight to his lady. When they walked along the street, he was careful to be on the outside,—somewhere he had heard that this was the proper thing to do,—and when a crossing to the opposite side of the street put him on the inside, he swiftly side-stepped behind her to gain the outside again. He carried her parcels for her, and once, when rain threatened, her umbrella. He had never heard of the custom of sending flowers to one's lady-love, so he sent Genevieve fruit instead. There was utility in fruit. It was good to eat. Flowers never entered his mind, until, one day, he noticed a pale rose in her hair. It drew his gaze again and again. It was her hair, therefore the presence of the flower interested him. Again, it interested him because she had chosen to put it there. For these reasons he was led to observe the rose more closely. He discovered that the effect in itself was beautiful, and it fascinated him. His ingenuous delight in it was a delight to her, and a new and mutual love-thrill was theirs—because of a flower. Straightway he became a lover of flowers. Also, he became an inventor in gallantry. He sent her a bunch of violets. The idea was his own. He had never heard of a man sending flowers to a woman. Flowers were used for decorative purposes, also for funerals. He sent Genevieve flowers nearly every day, and so far as he was concerned the idea was original, as positive an invention as ever arose in the mind of man.

He was tremulous in his devotion to her—as tremulous as was she in her reception of him. She was all that was pure and good, a holy of holies not lightly to be profaned even by what might possibly be the too ardent reverence of a devotee. She was a being wholly different from any he had ever known. She was not as other girls. It never entered his head that she was of the same clay as his own sisters, or anybody's sister. She was more than mere girl, than mere woman. She was—well, she was Genevieve, a being of a class by herself, nothing less than a miracle of creation.

And for her, in turn, there was in him but little less of illusion. Her judgment of him in minor things might be critical (while his judgment of her was sheer worship, and had in it nothing critical at all); but in her judgment of him as a whole she forgot the sum of the parts, and knew him only as a creature of wonder, who gave meaning to life, and for whom she could die as willingly as she could live. She often beguiled her waking dreams of him with fancied situations, wherein, dying for him, she at last adequately expressed the love she felt for him, and which, living, she knew she could never fully express.

Their love was all fire and dew. The physical scarcely entered into it, for such seemed profanation. The ultimate physical facts of their relation were something which they never considered. Yet the immediate physical facts they knew, the immediate yearnings and raptures of the flesh—the touch of finger tips on hand or arm, the momentary pressure of a hand-clasp, the rare lip-caress of a kiss, the tingling thrill of her hair upon his cheek, of her hand lightly thrusting back the locks from above his eyes. All this they knew, but also, and they knew not why, there seemed a hint of sin about these caresses and sweet bodily contacts.

There were times when she felt impelled to throw her arms around him in a very abandonment of love, but always some sanctity restrained her. At such moments she was distinctly and unpleasantly aware of some unguessed sin that lurked within her. It was wrong, undoubtedly wrong, that she should wish to caress her lover in so unbecoming a fashion. No self-respecting girl could dream of doing such a thing. It was unwomanly. Besides, if she had done it, what would he have thought of it? And while she contemplated so horrible a catastrophe, she seemed to shrivel and wilt in a furnace of secret shame.

Nor did Joe escape the prick of curious desires, chiefest among which, perhaps, was the desire to hurt Genevieve. When, after long and tortuous degrees, he had achieved the bliss of putting his arm round her waist, he felt spasmodic impulses to make the embrace crushing, till she should cry out with the hurt. It was not his nature to wish to hurt any living thing. Even in the ring, to hurt was never the intention of any blow he struck. In such case he played the Game, and the goal of the Game was to down an antagonist and keep that antagonist down for a space of ten seconds. So he never struck merely to hurt; the hurt was incidental to the end, and the end was quite another matter. And yet here, with this girl he loved, came the desire to hurt. Why, when with thumb and forefinger he had ringed her wrist, he should desire to contract that ring till it crushed, was beyond him. He could not understand, and felt that he was discovering depths of brutality in his nature of which he had never dreamed.

Once, on parting, he threw his arms around her and swiftly drew her against him. Her gasping cry of surprise and pain brought him to his senses and left him there very much embarrassed and still trembling with a vague and nameless delight. And she, too, was trembling. In the hurt itself, which was the essence of the vigorous embrace, she had found delight; and again she knew sin, though she knew not its nature nor why it should be sin.

Came the day, very early in their walking out, when Silverstein chanced upon Joe in his store and stared at him with saucer-eyes. Came likewise the scene, after Joe had departed, when the maternal feelings of Mrs. Silverstein found vent in a diatribe against all prize-fighters and against Joe Fleming in particular. Vainly had Silverstein striven to stay the spouse's wrath. There was need for her wrath. All the maternal feelings were hers but none of the maternal rights.

Genevieve was aware only of the diatribe; she knew a flood of abuse was pouring from the lips of the Jewess, but she was too stunned to hear the details of the abuse. Joe, her Joe, was Joe Fleming the prize-fighter. It was abhorrent, impossible, too grotesque to be believable. Her clear-eyed, girl-cheeked Joe might be anything but a prize-fighter. She had never seen one, but he in no way resembled her conception of what a prize-fighter must be—the human brute with tiger eyes and a streak for a forehead. Of course she had heard of Joe Fleming—who in West Oakland had not?—but that there should be anything more than a coincidence of names had never crossed her mind.

She came out of her daze to hear Mrs. Silverstein's hysterical sneer, "keepin' company vit a bruiser." Next, Silverstein and his wife fell to differing on "noted" and "notorious" as applicable to her lover.

"But he iss a good boy," Silverstein was contending. "He make der money, an' he safe der money."

"You tell me dat!" Mrs. Silverstein screamed. "Vat you know? You know too much. You spend good money on der prize-fighters. How you know? Tell me dat! How you know?"

"I know vat I know," Silverstein held on sturdily—a thing Genevieve had never before seen him do when his wife was in her tantrums. "His fader die, he go to work in Hansen's sail-loft. He haf six brudders an' sisters younger as he iss. He iss der liddle fader. He vork hard, all der time. He buy der pread an' der meat, an' pay der rent. On Saturday night he bring home ten dollar. Den Hansen gif him twelve dollar—vat he do? He iss der liddle fader, he bring it home to der mudder. He vork all der time, he get twenty dollar—vat he do? He bring it home. Der liddle brudders an' sisters go to school, vear good clothes, haf better pread an' meat; der mudder lif fat, dere iss joy in der eye, an' she iss proud of her good boy Joe.

"But he haf der beautiful body—ach, Gott, der beautiful body!—stronger as der ox, k-vicker as der tiger-cat, der head cooler as der ice-box, der eyes vat see eferytings, k-vick, just like dat. He put on der gloves vit der boys at Hansen's loft, he put on der gloves vit de boys at der varehouse. He go before der club; he knock out der Spider, k-vick, one punch, just like dat, der first time. Der purse iss five dollar—vat he do? He bring it home to der mudder.

"He go many times before der clubs; he get many purses—ten dollar, fifty dollar, one hundred dollar. Vat he do? Tell me dat! Quit der job at Hansen's? Haf der good time vit der boys? No, no; he iss der good boy. He vork efery day. He fight at night before der clubs. He say, 'Vat for I pay der rent, Silverstein?'—to me, Silverstein, he say dat. Nefer mind vat I say, but he buy der good house for der mudder. All der time he vork at Hansen's and fight before der clubs to pay for der house. He buy der piano for der sisters, der carpets, der pictures on der vall. An' he iss all der time straight. He bet on himself—dat iss der good sign. Ven der man bets on himself dat is der time you bet too—"

Here Mrs. Silverstein groaned her horror of gambling, and her husband, aware that his eloquence had betrayed him, collapsed into voluble assurances that he was ahead of the game. "An' all because of Joe Fleming," he concluded. "I back him efery time to vin."

But Genevieve and Joe were preëminently mated, and nothing, not even this terrible discovery, could keep them apart. In vain Genevieve tried to steel herself against him; but she fought herself, not him. To her surprise she discovered a thousand excuses for him, found him lovable as ever; and she entered into his life to be his destiny, and to control him after the way of women. She saw his future and hers through glowing vistas of reform, and her first great deed was when she wrung from him his promise to cease fighting.

And he, after the way of men, pursuing the dream of love and striving for possession of the precious and deathless object of desire, had yielded. And yet, in the very moment of promising her, he knew vaguely, deep down, that he could never abandon the Game; that somewhere, sometime, in the future, he must go back to it. And he had had a swift vision of his mother and brothers and sisters, their multitudinous wants, the house with its painting and repairing, its street assessments and taxes, and of the coming of children to him and Genevieve, and of his own daily wage in the sail-making loft. But the next moment the vision was dismissed, as such warnings are always dismissed, and he saw before him only Genevieve, and he knew only his hunger for her and the call of his being to her; and he accepted calmly her calm assumption of his life and actions.

He was twenty, she was eighteen, boy and girl, the pair of them, and made for progeny, healthy and normal, with steady blood pounding through their bodies; and wherever they went together, even on Sunday outings across the bay amongst people who did not know him, eyes were continually drawn to them. He matched her girl's beauty with his boy's beauty, her grace with his strength, her delicacy of line and fibre with the harsher vigor and muscle of the male. Frank-faced, fresh-colored, almost ingenuous in expression, eyes blue and wide apart, he drew and held the gaze of more than one woman far above him in the social scale. Of such glances and dim maternal promptings he was quite unconscious, though Genevieve was quick to see and understand; and she knew each time the pang of a fierce joy in that he was hers and that she held him in the hollow of her hand. He did see, however, and rather resented, the men's glances drawn by her. These, too, she saw and understood as he did not dream of understanding.

CHAPTER 3

GENEVIEVE SLIPPED ON A PAIR of Joe's shoes, light-soled and dapper, and laughed with Lottie, who stooped to turn up the trousers for her. Lottie was his sister, and in the secret. To her was due the inveigling of his mother into making a neighborhood call so that they could have the house to themselves. They went down into the kitchen where Joe was waiting. His face brightened as he came to meet her, love shining frankly forth.

"Now get up those skirts, Lottie," he commanded. "Haven't any time to waste. There, that'll do. You see, you only want the bottoms of the pants to show. The coat will cover the rest. Now let's see how it'll fit.

"Borrowed it from Chris; he's a dead sporty sport—little, but oh, my!" he went on, helping Genevieve into an overcoat which fell to her heels and which fitted her as a tailor-made overcoat should fit the man for whom it is made.

Joe put a cap on her head and turned up the collar, which was generous to exaggeration, meeting the cap and completely hiding her hair. When he buttoned the collar in front, its points served to cover the cheeks, chin and mouth were buried in its depths, and a close scrutiny revealed only shadowy eyes and a little less shadowy nose. She walked across the room, the bottom of the trousers just showing as the bang of the coat was disturbed by movement.

"A sport with a cold and afraid of catching more, all right all right," the boy laughed, proudly surveying his handiwork. "How much money you got? I'm layin' ten to six. Will you take the short end?"

"Who's short?" she asked.

"Ponta, of course," Lottie blurted out her hurt, as though there could be any question of it even for an instant.

"Of course," Genevieve said sweetly, "only I don't know much about such things."

This time Lottie kept her lips together, but the new hurt showed on her face. Joe looked at his watch and said it was time to go. His sister's arms went about his neck, and she kissed him soundly on the lips. She kissed Genevieve, too, and saw them to the gate, one arm of her brother about her waist.

"What does ten to six mean?" Genevieve asked, the while their footfalls rang out on the frosty air.

"That I'm the long end, the favorite," he answered. "That a man bets ten dollars at the ring side that I win against six dollars another man is betting that I lose."

"But if you're the favorite and everybody thinks you'll win, how does anybody bet against you?"

"That's what makes prize-fighting—difference of opinion," he laughed. "Besides, there's always the chance of a lucky punch, an accident. Lots of chance," he said gravely.

She shrank against him, clingingly and protectingly, and he laughed with surety.

"You wait, and you'll see. An' don't get scared at the start. The first few rounds'll be something fierce. That's Ponta's strong point. He's a wild man, with an kinds of punches,—a whirlwind,—and he gets his man in the first rounds. He's put away a whole lot of cleverer and better men than him. It's up to me to live through it, that's all. Then he'll be all in. Then I go after him, just watch. You'll know when I go after him, an' I'll get'm, too."

They came to the hall, on a dark street-corner, ostensibly the quarters of an athletic club, but in reality an institution designed for pulling off fights and keeping within the police ordinance. Joe drew away from her, and they walked apart to the entrance.

"Keep your hands in your pockets whatever you do," Joe warned her, "and it'll be all right. Only a couple of minutes of it."

"He's with me," Joe said to the door-keeper, who was talking with a policeman.

Both men greeted him familiarly, taking no notice of his companion.

"They never tumbled; nobody'll tumble," Joe assured her, as they climbed the stairs to the second story. "And even if they did, they wouldn't know who it was and they's keep it mum for me. Here, come in here!"

He whisked her into a little office-like room and left her seated on a dusty, broken-bottomed chair. A few minutes later he was back again, clad in a long bath robe, canvas shoes on his feet. She began to tremble against him, and his arm passed gently around her.

"It'll be all right, Genevieve," he said encouragingly. "I've got it all fixed. Nobody'll tumble."

"It's you, Joe," she said. "I don't care for myself. It's you."

"Don't care for yourself! But that's what I thought you were afraid of!"

He looked at her in amazement, the wonder of woman bursting upon him in a more transcendent glory than ever, and he had seen much of the wonder of woman in Genevieve. He was speechless for a moment, and then stammered:—

"You mean me? And you don't care what people think? or anything?—or anything?"

A sharp double knock at the door, and a sharper "Get a move on yerself, Joe!" brought him back to immediate things.

"Quick, one last kiss, Genevieve," he whispered, almost holily. "It's my last fight, an' I'll fight as never before with you lookin' at me."

The next she knew, the pressure of his lips yet warm on hers, she was in a group of jostling young fellows, none of whom seemed to take the slightest notice of her. Several had their coats off and their shirt sleeves rolled up. They entered the hall from the rear, still keeping the casual formation of the group, and moved slowly up a side aisle.

It was a crowded, ill-lighted hall, barn-like in its proportions, and the smoke-laden air gave a peculiar distortion to everything. She felt as though she would stifle.

There were shrill cries of boys selling programmes and soda water, and there was a great bass rumble of masculine voices. She heard a voice offering ten to six on Joe Fleming. The utterance was monotonous—hopeless, it seemed to her, and she felt a quick thrill. It was her Joe against whom everybody was to bet.

And she felt other thrills. Her blood was touched, as by fire, with romance, adventure—the unknown, the mysterious, the terrible—as she penetrated this haunt of men where women came not. And there were other thrills. It was the only time in her life she had dared the rash thing. For the first time she was overstepping the bounds laid down by that harshest of tyrants, the Mrs. Grundy of the working class. She felt fear, and for herself, though the moment before she had been thinking only of Joe.

Before she knew it, the front of the hall had been reached, and she had gone up half a dozen steps into a small dressing-room. This was crowded to suffocation—by men who played the Game, she concluded, in one capacity or another. And here she lost Joe. But before the real personal fright could soundly clutch her, one of the young fellows said gruffly, "Come along with me, you," and as she wedged out at his heels she noticed that another one of the escort was following her.

They came upon a sort of stage, which accommodated three rows of men; and she caught her first glimpse of the squared ring. She was on a level with it, and so near that she could have reached out and touched its ropes. She noticed that it was covered with padded canvas. Beyond the ring, and on either side, as in a fog, she could see the crowded house.

The dressing-room she had left abutted upon one corner of the ring. Squeezing her way after her guide through the seated men, she crossed the end of the hall and entered a similar dressing-room at the other corner of the ring.

"Now don't make a noise, and stay here till I come for you," instructed her guide, pointing out a peep-hole arrangement in the wall of the room.

Chapter 4

SHE HURRIED TO the peep-hole, and found herself against the ring. She could see the whole of it, though part of the audience was shut off. The ring was well lighted by an overhead cluster of patent gas-burners. The front row of the men she had squeezed past, because of their paper and pencils, she decided to be reporters from the local papers up-town. One of them was chewing gum. Behind them, on the other two rows of seats, she could make out firemen from the near-by engine-house and several policemen in uniform. In the middle of the front row, flanked by the reporters, sat the young chief of police. She was startled by catching sight of Mr. Clausen on the opposite side of the ring. There he sat, austere, side-whiskered, pink and white, close up against the front of the ring. Several seats farther on, in the same front row, she discovered Silverstein, his weazen features glowing with anticipation.

A few cheers heralded the advent of several young fellows, in shirt-sleeves, carrying buckets, bottles, and towels, who crawled through the ropes and crossed to the diagonal corner from her. One of them sat down on a stool and leaned back against the ropes. She saw that he was bare-legged, with canvas shoes on his feet, and that his body was swathed in a heavy white sweater. In the meantime another group had occupied the corner directly against her. Louder cheers drew her attention to it, and she saw Joe seated on a stool still clad in the bath robe, his short chestnut curls within a yard of her eyes.

A young man, in a black suit, with a mop of hair and a preposterously tall starched collar, walked to the centre of the ring and held up his hand.

"Gentlemen will please stop smoking," he said.

His effort was applauded by groans and cat-calls, and she noticed with indignation that nobody stopped smoking. Mr. Clausen held a burning match in his fingers while the announcement was being made, and then calmly lighted his cigar. She felt that she hated him in that moment. How was her Joe to fight in such an atmosphere? She could scarcely breathe herself, and she was only sitting down.

The announcer came over to Joe. He stood up. His bath robe fell away from him, and he stepped forth to the centre of the ring, naked save for the low canvas shoes and a narrow hip-cloth of white. Genevieve's eyes dropped. She sat alone, with none to see, but her face was burning with shame at sight of the beautiful nakedness of her lover. But she looked again, guiltily, for the joy that was hers in beholding what she knew must be sinful to behold. The leap of something within her and the stir of her being toward him must be sinful. But it was delicious sin, and she did not deny her eyes. In vain Mrs. Grundy admonished her. The pagan in her, original sin, and all nature urged her on. The mothers of all the past were whispering through her, and there was a clamour of the children unborn. But of this she knew nothing. She knew only that it was sin, and she lifted her head proudly, recklessly resolved, in one great surge of revolt, to sin to the uttermost.

She had never dreamed of the form under the clothes. The form, beyond the hands and the face, had no part in her mental processes. A child of garmented civilization, the garment was to her the form. The race of men was to her a race of garmented bipeds, with hands and faces and hair-covered heads. When she thought of Joe, the Joe instantly visualized on her mind was a clothed Joe—girl-cheeked, blue-eyed, curly-headed, but clothed. And there he stood, all but naked, godlike, in a white blaze of light. She had never conceived of the form of God except as nebulously naked, and the thought-association was startling. It seemed to her that her sin partook of sacrilege or blasphemy.

Her chromo-trained æsthetic sense exceeded its education and told her that here were beauty and wonder. She had always liked the physical presentment of Joe, but it was a presentment of clothes, and she had thought the pleasingness of it due to the neatness and taste with which he dressed. She had never dreamed that this lurked beneath. It dazzled her. His skin was fair as a woman's, far more satiny, and no rudimentary hair-growth marred its white lustre. This she perceived, but all the rest, the perfection of line and strength and development, gave pleasure without her knowing why. There was a cleanness and grace about it. His face was like a cameo, and his lips, parted in a smile, made it very boyish.

He smiled as he faced the audience, when the announcer, placing a hand on his shoulder, said: "Joe Fleming, the Pride of West Oakland."

Cheers and hand-clappings stormed up, and she heard affectionate cries of "Oh, you, Joe!" Men shouted it at him again and again.

He walked back to his corner. Never to her did he seem less a fighter than then. His eyes were too mild; there was not a spark of the beast in them, nor in his face, while his body seemed too fragile, what of its fairness and smoothness, and his face too boyish and sweet-tempered and intelligent. She did not have the expert's eye for the depth of chest, the wide nostrils, the recuperative lungs, and the muscles under their satin sheaths—crypts of energy wherein lurked the chemistry of destruction. To her he looked like a something of Dresden china, to be handled gently and with care, liable to be shattered to fragments by the first rough touch.

John Ponta, stripped of his white sweater by the pulling and hauling of two of his seconds, came to the centre of the ring. She knew terror as she looked at him. Here was the fighter—the beast with a streak for a forehead, with beady eyes under lowering and bushy brows, flat-nosed, thick-lipped, sullen-mouthed. He was heavy-jawed, bull-necked, and the short, straight hair of the head seemed to her frightened eyes the stiff bristles on a hog's back. Here were coarseness and brutishness—a thing savage, primordial, ferocious. He was swarthy to blackness, and his body was covered with a hairy growth that matted like a dog's on his chest and shoulders. He was deep-chested, thick-legged, large-muscled, but unshapely. His muscles were knots, and he was gnarled and knobby, twisted out of beauty by excess of strength.

"John Ponta, West Bay Athletic Club," said the announcer.

A much smaller volume of cheers greeted him. It was evident that the crowd favored Joe with its sympathy.

"Go in an' eat 'm, Ponta! Eat 'm up!" a voice shouted in the lull.

This was received by scornful cries and groans. He did not like it, for his sullen mouth twisted into a half-snarl as he went back to his corner. He was too decided an atavism to draw the crowd's admiration. Instinctively the crowd disliked him. He was an animal, lacking in intelligence and spirit, a menace and a thing of fear, as the tiger and the snake are menaces and things of fear, better behind the bars of a cage than running free in the open.

And he felt that the crowd had no relish for him. He was like an animal in the circle of its enemies, and he turned and glared at them with malignant eyes. Little Silverstein, shouting out Joe's name with high glee, shrank away from Ponta's gaze, shrivelled as in fierce heat, the sound gurgling and dying in his throat. Genevieve saw the little by-play, and as Ponta's eyes slowly swept round the circle of their hate and met hers, she, too, shrivelled and shrank back. The next moment they were past, pausing to centre long on Joe. It seemed to her that Ponta was working himself into a rage.

Joe returned the gaze with mild boy's eyes, but his face grew serious.

The announcer escorted a third man to the centre of the ring, a genial-faced young fellow in shirt-sleeves.

"Eddy Jones, who will referee this contest," said the announcer.

"Oh, you, Eddy!" men shouted in the midst of the applause, and it was apparent to Genevieve that he, too, was well beloved.

Both men were being helped into the gloves by their seconds, and one of Ponta's seconds came over and examined the gloves before they went on Joe's hands. The referee called them to the centre of the ring. The seconds followed, and they made quite a group, Joe and Ponta facing each other, the referee in the middle, the seconds leaning with hands on one another's shoulders, their heads craned forward. The referee was talking, and all listened attentively.

The group broke up. Again the announcer came to the front.

"Joe Fleming fights at one hundred and twenty-eight," he said; "John Ponta at one hundred and forty. They will fight as long as one hand is free, and take care of themselves in the breakaway. The audience must remember that a decision must be given. There are no draws fought before this club."

He crawled through the ropes and dropped from the ring to the floor. There was a scuttling in the corners as the seconds cleared out through the ropes, taking with them the stools and buckets. Only remained in the ring the two fighters and the referee. A gong sounded. The two men advanced rapidly to the centre. Their right hands extended and for a fraction of an instant met in a perfunctory shake. Then Ponta lashed out, savagely, right and left, and Joe escaped by springing back. Like a projectile, Ponta hurled himself after him and upon him.

The fight was on. Genevieve clutched one hand to her breast and watched. She was bewildered by the swiftness and savagery of Ponta's assault, and by the multitude of blows he struck. She felt that Joe was surely being destroyed. At times she could not see his face, so obscured was it by the flying gloves. But she could hear the resounding blows, and with the sound of each blow she felt a sickening sensation in the pit of her stomach. She did not know that what she heard was the impact of glove on glove, or glove on shoulder, and that no damage was being done.

She was suddenly aware that a change had come over the fight. Both men were clutching each other in a tense embrace; no blows were being struck at all. She recognized it to be what Joe had described to her as the "clinch." Ponta was struggling to free himself, Joe was holding on.

The referee shouted, "Break!" Joe made an effort to get away, but Ponta got one hand free and Joe rushed back into a second clinch, to escape the blow. But this time, she noticed, the heel of his glove was pressed against Ponta's mouth and chin, and at the second "Break!" of the referee, Joe shoved his opponent's head back and sprang clear himself.

For a brief several seconds she had an unobstructed view of her lover. Left foot a trifle advanced, knees slightly bent, he was crouching, with his head drawn well down between his shoulders and shielded by them. His hands were in position before him, ready either to attack or defend. The muscles of his body were tense, and as he moved about she could see them bunch up and writhe and crawl like live things under the white skin.

But again Ponta was upon him and he was struggling to live. He crouched a bit more, drew his body more compactly together, and covered up with his hands, elbows, and forearms. Blows rained upon him, and it looked to her as though he were being beaten to death.

But he was receiving the blows on his gloves and shoulders, rocking back and forth to the force of them like a tree in a storm, while the house cheered its delight. It was not until she understood this applause, and saw Silverstein half out of his seat and intensely, madly happy, and heard the "Oh, you, Joe's!" from many throats, that she realized that instead of being cruelly punished he was acquitting himself well. Then he would emerge for a moment, again to be enveloped and hidden in the whirlwind of Ponta's ferocity.

CHAPTER 5

THE GONG SOUNDED. It seemed they had been fighting half an hour, though from what Joe had told her she knew it had been only three minutes. With the crash of the gong Joe's seconds were through the ropes and running him into his corner for the blessed minute of rest. One man, squatting on the floor between his outstretched feet and elevating them by resting them on his knees, was violently chafing his legs. Joe sat on the stool, leaning far back into the corner, head thrown back and arms outstretched on the ropes to give easy expansion to the chest. With wide-open mouth he was breathing the towel-driven air furnished by two of the seconds, while listening to the counsel of still another second who talked with low voice in his ear and at the same time sponged off his face, shoulders, and chest.

Hardly had all this been accomplished (it had taken no more than several seconds), when the gong sounded, the seconds scuttled through the ropes with their paraphernalia, and Joe and Ponta were advancing against each other to the centre of the ring. Genevieve had no idea that a minute could be so short. For a moment she felt that this rest had been cut, and was suspicious of she knew not what.

Ponta lashed out, right and left, savagely as ever, and though Joe blocked the blows, such was the force of them that he was knocked backward several steps. Ponta was after him with the spring of a tiger. In the involuntary effort to maintain equilibrium, Joe had uncovered himself, flinging one arm out and lifting his head from beneath the sheltering shoulders. So swiftly had Ponta followed him, that a terrible swinging blow was coming at his unguarded jaw. He ducked forward and down, Ponta's fist just missing the back of his head. As he came back to the perpendicular, Ponta's left fist drove at him in a straight punch that would have knocked him backward through the ropes. Again, and with a swiftness an inappreciable fraction of time quicker than Ponta's, he ducked forward. Ponta's fist grazed the backward slope of the shoulder, and glanced off into the air. Ponta's right drove straight out, and the graze was repeated as Joe ducked into the safety of a clinch.

Genevieve sighed with relief, her tense body relaxing and a faintness coming over her. The crowd was cheering madly. Silverstein was on his feet, shouting, gesticulating, completely out of himself. And even Mr. Clausen was yelling his enthusiasm, at the top of his lungs, into the ear of his nearest neighbor.

The clinch was broken and the fight went on. Joe blocked, and backed, and slid around the ring, avoiding blows and living somehow through the whirlwind onslaughts. Rarely did he strike blows himself, for Ponta had a quick eye and could defend as well as attack, while Joe had no chance against the other's enormous vitality. His hope lay in that Ponta himself should ultimately consume his strength.

But Genevieve was beginning to wonder why her lover did not fight. She grew angry. She wanted to see him wreak vengeance on this beast that had persecuted him so. Even as she waxed impatient, the chance came, and Joe whipped his fist to Ponta's mouth. It was a staggering blow. She saw Ponta's head go back with a jerk and the quick dye of blood upon his lips. The blow, and the great shout from the audience, angered him. He rushed like a wild man. The fury of his previous assaults was as nothing compared with the fury of this one. And there was no more opportunity for another blow. Joe was too busy living through the storm he had already caused, blocking, covering up, and ducking into the safety and respite of the clinches.

But the clinch was not all safety and respite. Every instant of it was intense watchfulness, while the breakaway was still more dangerous. Genevieve had noticed, with a slight touch of amusement, the curious way in which Joe snuggled his body in against Ponta's in the clinches; but she had not realized why, until, in one such clinch, before the snuggling in could be effected, Ponta's fist whipped straight up in the air from under, and missed Joe's chin by a hair's-breadth. In another and later clinch, when she had already relaxed and sighed her relief at seeing him safely snuggled, Ponta, his chin over Joe's shoulder, lifted his right arm and struck a terrible downward blow on the small of the back. The crowd groaned its apprehension, while Joe quickly locked his opponent's arms to prevent a repetition of the blow.

The gong struck, and after the fleeting minute of rest, they went at it again—in Joe's corner, for Ponta had made a rush to meet him clear across the ring. Where the blow had been over the kidneys, the white skin had become bright red. This splash of color, the size of the glove, fascinated and frightened Genevieve so that she could scarcely take her eyes from it. Promptly, in the next clinch, the blow was repeated; but after that Joe usually managed to give Ponta the heel of the glove on the mouth and so hold his head back. This prevented the striking of the blow; but three times more, before the round ended, Ponta effected the trick, each time striking the same vulnerable part.

Another rest and another round went by, with no further damage to Joe and no diminution of strength on the part of Ponta. But in the beginning of the fifth round, Joe, caught in a corner, made as though to duck into a clinch. Just before it was effected, and at the precise moment that Ponta was ready with his own body to receive the snuggling in of Joe's body, Joe drew back slightly and drove with his fists at his opponent's unprotected stomach. Lightning-like blows they were, four of them, right and left; and heavy they were, for Ponta winced away from them and staggered back, half dropping his arms, his shoulders drooping forward and in, as though he were about to double in at the waist and collapse. Joe's quick eye saw the opening, and he smashed straight out upon Ponta's mouth, following instantly with a half swing, half hook, for the jaw. It missed, striking the cheek instead, and sending Ponta staggering sideways.

The house was on its feet, shouting, to a man. Genevieve could hear men crying, "He's got 'm, he's got 'm!" and it seemed to her the beginning of the end. She, too, was out of herself; softness and tenderness had vanished; she exulted with each crushing blow her lover delivered.

But Ponta's vitality was yet to be reckoned with. As, like a tiger, he had followed Joe up, Joe now followed him up. He made another half swing, half hook, for Ponta's jaw, and Ponta, already recovering his wits and strength, ducked cleanly. Joe's fist passed on through empty air, and so great was the momentum of the blow that it carried him around, in a half twirl, sideways. Then Ponta lashed out with his left. His glove landed on Joe's unguarded neck. Genevieve saw her lover's arms drop to his sides as his body lifted, went backward, and fell limply to the floor. The referee, bending over him, began to count the seconds, emphasizing the passage of each second with a downward sweep of his right arm.

The audience was still as death. Ponta had partly turned to the house to receive the approval that was his due, only to be met by this chill, graveyard silence. Quick wrath surged up in him. It was unfair. His opponent only was applauded—if he struck a blow, if he escaped a blow; he, Ponta, who had forced the fighting from the start, had received no word of cheer.

His eyes blazed as he gathered himself together and sprang to his prostrate foe. He crouched alongside of him, right arm drawn back and ready for a smashing blow the instant Joe should start to rise. The referee, still bending over and counting with his right hand, shoved Ponta back with his left. The latter, crouching, circled around, and the referee circled with him, thrusting him back and keeping between him and the fallen man.

"Four—five—six—" the count went on, and Joe, rolling over on his face, squirmed weakly to draw himself to his knees. This he succeeded in doing, resting on one knee, a hand to the floor on either side and the other leg bent under him to help him rise. "Take the count! Take the count!" a dozen voices rang out from the audience.

"For God's sake, take the count!" one of Joe's seconds cried warningly from the edge of the ring. Genevieve gave him one swift glance, and saw the young fellow's face, drawn and white, his lips unconsciously moving as he kept the count with the referee.

"Seven—eight—nine—" the seconds went.

The ninth sounded and was gone, when the referee gave Ponta a last backward shove and Joe came to his feet, bunched up, covered up, weak, but cool, very cool. Ponta hurled himself upon him with terrific force, delivering an uppercut and a straight punch. But Joe blocked the two, ducked a third, stepped to the side to avoid a fourth, and was then driven backward into a corner by a hurricane of blows. He was exceedingly weak. He tottered as he kept his footing, and staggered back and forth. His back was against the ropes. There was no further retreat. Ponta paused, as if to make doubly sure, then feinted with his left and struck fiercely with his right with all his strength. But Joe ducked into a clinch and was for a moment saved.

Ponta struggled frantically to free himself. He wanted to give the finish to this foe already so far gone. But

Joe was holding on for life, resisting the other's every effort, as fast as one hold or grip was torn loose finding a new one by which to cling. "Break!" the referee commanded. Joe held on tighter. "Make 'm break! Why the hell don't you make 'm break?" Ponta panted at the referee. Again the latter commanded the break. Joe refused, keeping, as he well knew, within his rights. Each moment of the clinch his strength was coming back to him, his brain was clearing, the cobwebs were disappearing from before his eyes. The round was young, and he must live, somehow, through the nearly three minutes of it yet to run.

The referee clutched each by the shoulder and sundered them violently, passing quickly between them as he thrust them backward in order to make a clean break of it. The moment he was free, Ponta sprang at Joe like a wild animal bearing down its prey. But Joe covered up, blocked, and fell into a clinch. Again Ponta struggled to get free, Joe held on, and the referee thrust them apart. And again Joe avoided damage and clinched.

Genevieve realized that in the clinches he was not being beaten—why, then, did not the referee let him hold on? It was cruel. She hated the genial-faced Eddy Jones in those moments, and she partly rose from her chair, her hands clenched with anger, the nails cutting into the palms till they hurt. The rest of the round, the three long minutes of it, was a succession of clinches and breaks. Not once did Ponta succeed in striking his opponent the deadly final blow. And Ponta was like a madman, raging because of his impotency in the face of his helpless and all but vanquished foe. One blow, only one blow, and he could not deliver it!

Joe's ring experience and coolness saved him. With shaken consciousness and trembling body, he clutched and held on, while the ebbing life turned and flooded up in him again. Once, in his passion, unable to hit him, Ponta made as though to lift him up and hurl him to the floor.

"V'y don't you bite him?" Silverstein taunted shrilly.

In the stillness the sally was heard over the whole house, and the audience, relieved of its anxiety for its favorite, laughed with an uproariousness that had in it the note of hysteria. Even Genevieve felt that there was something irresistibly funny in the remark, and the relief of the audience was communicated to her; yet she felt sick and faint, and was overwrought with horror at what she had seen and was seeing.

"Bite 'm!   Bite 'm!" voices from the recovered audience were shouting. "Chew his ear off, Ponta! That's the only way you can get 'm! Eat 'm up! Eat 'm up! Oh, why don't you eat 'm up?"

The effect was bad on Ponta. He became more frenzied than ever, and more impotent. He panted and sobbed, wasting his effort by too much effort, losing sanity and control and futilely trying to compensate for the loss by excess of physical endeavor. He knew only the blind desire to destroy, shook Joe in the clinches as a terrier might a rat, strained and struggled for freedom of body and arms, and all the while Joe calmly clutched and held on. The referee worked manfully and fairly to separate them. Perspiration ran down his face. It took all his strength to split those clinging bodies, and no sooner had he split them than Joe fell unharmed into another embrace and the work had to be done all over again. In vain, when freed, did Ponta try to avoid the clutching arms and twining body. He could not keep away. He had to come close in order to strike, and each time Joe baffled him and caught him in his arms.

And Genevieve, crouched in the little dressing-room and peering through the peep-hole, was baffled, too. She was an interested party in what seemed a death-struggle—was not one of the fighters her Joe?—but the audience understood and she did not. The Game had not unveiled to her. The lure of it was beyond her. It was greater mystery than ever. She could not comprehend its power. What delight could there be for Joe in that brutal surging and straining of bodies, those fierce clutches, fiercer blows, and terrible hurts? Surely, she, Genevieve, offered more than that—rest, and content, and sweet, calm joy. Her bid for the heart of him and the soul of him was finer and more generous than the bid of the Game; yet he dallied with both—held her in his arms, but turned his head to listen to that other and siren call she could not understand.

The gong struck. The round ended with a break in Ponta's corner. The white-faced young second was through the ropes with the first clash of sound. He seized Joe in his arms, lifted him clear of the floor, and ran with him across the ring to his own corner. His seconds worked over him furiously, chafing his legs, slapping his abdomen, stretching the hip-cloth out with their fingers so that he might breathe more easily. For the first time Genevieve saw the stomach-breathing of a man, an abdomen that rose and fell far more with every breath than her breast rose and fell after she had run for a car. The pungency of ammonia bit her nostrils, wafted to her from the soaked sponge wherefrom he breathed the fiery fumes that cleared his brain. He gargled his mouth and throat, took a suck at a divided lemon, and all the while the towels worked like mad, driving oxygen into his lungs to purge the pounding blood and send it back revivified for the struggle yet to come. His heated body was sponged with water, doused with it, and bottles were turned mouth-downward on his head.

CHAPTER 6

THE GONG FOR THE SIXTH ROUND struck, and both men advanced to meet each other, their bodies glistening with water. Ponta rushed two-thirds of the way across the ring, so intent was he on getting at his man before full recovery could be effected. But Joe had lived through. He was strong again, and getting stronger. He blocked several vicious blows and then smashed back, sending Ponta reeling. He attempted to follow up, but wisely forbore and contented himself with blocking and covering up in the whirlwind his blow had raised.

The fight was as it had been at the beginning—Joe protecting, Ponta rushing. But Ponta was never at ease. He did not have it all his own way. At any moment, in his fiercest onslaughts, his opponent was liable to lash out and reach him. Joe saved his strength. He struck one blow to Ponta's ten, but his one blow rarely missed. Ponta overwhelmed him in the attacks, yet could do nothing with him, while Joe's tiger-like strokes, always imminent, compelled respect. They toned Ponta's ferocity. He was no longer able to go in with the complete abandon of destructiveness which had marked his earlier efforts.

But a change was coming over the fight. The audience was quick to note it, and even Genevieve saw it by the beginning of the ninth round. Joe was taking the offensive. In the clinches it was he who brought his fist down on the small of the back, striking the terrible kidney blow. He did it once, in each clinch, but with all his strength, and he did it every clinch. Then, in the breakaways, he began to uppercut Ponta on the stomach, or to hook his jaw or strike straight out upon the mouth. But at first sign of a coming of a whirlwind, Joe would dance nimbly away and cover up.

Two rounds of this went by, and three, but Ponta's strength, though perceptibly less, did not diminish rapidly. Joe's task was to wear down that strength, not with one blow, nor ten, but with blow after blow, without end, until that enormous strength should be beaten sheer out of its body. There was no rest for the man. Joe followed him up, step by step, his advancing left foot making an audible tap, tap, tap, on the hard canvas. Then there would come a sudden leap in, tiger-like, a blow struck, or blows, and a swift leap back, whereupon the left foot would take up again its tapping advance. When Ponta made his savage rushes, Joe carefully covered up, only to emerge, his left foot going tap, tap, tap, as he immediately followed up.

Ponta was slowly weakening. To the crowd the end was a foregone conclusion.

"Oh, you, Joe!" it yelled its admiration and affection.

"It's a shame to take the money!" it mocked. "Why don't you eat 'm, Ponta? Go on in an' eat 'm!"

In the one-minute intermissions Ponta's seconds worked over him as they had not worked before. Their calm trust in his tremendous vitality had been betrayed. Genevieve watched their excited efforts, while she listened to the white-faced second cautioning Joe.

"Take your time," he was saying. "You've got 'm, but you got to take your time. I've seen 'm fight. He's got a punch to the end of the count. I've seen 'm knocked out and clean batty, an' go on punching just the same. Mickey Sullivan had 'm goin'. Puts 'm to the mat as fast as he crawls up, six times, an' then leaves an opening. Ponta reaches for his jaw, an two minutes afterward Mickey's openin' his eyes an' askin' what's doin'. So you've got to watch 'm. No goin' in an' absorbin' one of them lucky punches, now. I got money on this fight, but I don't call it mine till he's counted out."

Ponta was being doused with water. As the gong sounded, one of his seconds inverted a water bottle on his head. He started toward the centre of the ring, and the second followed him for several steps, keeping the bottle still inverted. The referee shouted at him, and he fled the ring, dropping the bottle as he fled. It rolled over and over, the water gurgling out upon the canvas till the referee, with a quick flirt of his toe, sent the bottle rolling through the ropes.

In all the previous rounds Genevieve had not seen Joe's fighting face which had been prefigured to her that morning in the department store. Sometimes his face had been quite boyish; other times, when taking his fiercest punishment, it had been bleak and gray; and still later, when living through and clutching and holding on, it had taken on a wistful expression. But now, out of danger himself and as he forced the fight, his fighting face came upon him. She saw it and shuddered. It removed him so far from her. She had thought she knew him, all of him, and held him in the hollow of her hand; but this she did not know—this face of steel, this mouth of steel, these eyes of steel flashing the light and glitter of steel. It seemed to her the passionless face of an avenging angel, stamped only with the purpose of the Lord.

Ponta attempted one of his old-time rushes, but was stopped on the mouth. Implacable, insistent, ever menacing, never letting him rest, Joe followed him up. The round, the thirteenth, closed with a rush, in Ponta's corner. He attempted a rally, was brought to his knees, took the nine seconds' count, and then tried to clinch into safety, only to receive four of Joe's terrible stomach punches, so that with the gong he fell back, gasping, into the arms of his seconds.

Joe ran across the ring to his own corner.

"Now I'm going to get 'm," he said to his second.

"You sure fixed 'm that time," the latter answered. "Nothin' to stop you now but a lucky punch. Watch out for it."

Joe leaned forward, feet gathered under him for a spring, like a foot-racer waiting the start. He was waiting for the gong. When it sounded he shot forward and across the ring, catching Ponta in the midst of his seconds as he rose from his stool. And in the midst of his seconds he went down, knocked down by a right-hand blow. As he arose from the confusion of buckets, stools, and seconds, Joe put him down again. And yet a third time he went down before he could escape from his own corner.

Joe had at last become the whirlwind. Genevieve remembered his "just watch, you'll know when I go after him." The house knew it, too. It was on its feet, every voice raised in a fierce yell. It was the blood-cry of the crowd, and it sounded to her like what she imagined must be the howling of wolves. And what with confidence in her lover's victory she found room in her heart to pity Ponta.

In vain he struggled to defend himself, to block, to cover up, to duck, to clinch into a moment's safety. That moment was denied him. Knockdown after knockdown was his portion. He was knocked to the canvas backwards, and sideways, was punched in the clinches and in the breakaways—stiff, jolty blows that dazed his brain and drove the strength from his muscles. He was knocked into the corners and out again, against the ropes, rebounding, and with another blow against the ropes once more. He fanned the air with his arms, showering savage blows upon emptiness. There was nothing human left in him. He was the beast incarnate, roaring and raging and being destroyed. He was smashed down to his knees, but refused to take the count, staggering to his feet only to be met stiff-handed on the mouth and sent hurling back against the ropes.

In sore travail, gasping, reeling, panting, with glazing eyes and sobbing breath, grotesque and heroic, fighting to the last, striving to get at his antagonist, he surged and was driven about the ring. And in that moment Joe's foot slipped on the wet canvas. Ponta's swimming eyes saw and knew the chance. All the fleeing strength of his body gathered itself together for the lightning lucky punch. Even as Joe slipped the other smote him, fairly on the point of the chin. He went over backward. Genevieve saw his muscles relax while he was yet in the air, and she heard the thud of his head on the canvas.

The noise of the yelling house died suddenly. The referee, stooping over the inert body, was counting the seconds. Ponta tottered and fell to his knees. He struggled to his feet, swaying back and forth as he tried to sweep the audience with his hatred. His legs were trembling and bending under him; he was choking and sobbing, fighting to breathe. He reeled backward, and saved himself from falling by a blind clutching for the ropes. He clung there, drooping and bending and giving in all his body, his head upon his chest, until the referee counted the fatal tenth second and pointed to him in token that he had won.

He received no applause, and he squirmed through the ropes, snakelike, into the arms of his seconds, who helped him to the floor and supported him down the aisle into the crowd. Joe remained where he had fallen. His seconds carried him into his corner and placed him on the stool. Men began climbing into the ring, curious to see, but were roughly shoved out by the policemen, who were already there.

Genevieve looked on from her peep-hole. She was not greatly perturbed. Her lover had been knocked out. In so far as disappointment was his, she shared it with him; but that was all. She even felt glad in a way. The Game had played him false, and he was more surely hers. She had heard of knockouts from him. It often took men some time to recover from the effects. It was not till she heard the seconds asking for the doctor that she felt really worried.

They passed his limp body through the ropes to the stage, and it disappeared beyond the limits of her peep-hole. Then the door of her dressing-room was thrust open and a number of men came in. They were carrying Joe. He was laid down on the dusty floor, his head resting on the knee of one of the seconds. No one seemed surprised by her presence. She came over and knelt beside him. His eyes were closed, his lips slightly parted. His wet hair was plastered in straight locks about his face. She lifted one of his hands. It was very heavy, and the lifelessness of it shocked her. She looked suddenly at the faces of the seconds and of the men about her. They seemed frightened, all save one, and he was cursing, in a low voice, horribly. She looked up and saw Silverstein standing beside her. He, too, seemed frightened. He rested a kindly hand on her shoulder, tightening the fingers with a sympathetic pressure.

This sympathy frightened her. She began to feel dazed. There was a bustle as somebody entered the room. The person came forward, proclaiming irritably: "Get out! Get out! You've got to clear the room!"

A number of men silently obeyed.

"Who are you?" he abruptly demanded of Genevieve. "A girl, as I'm alive!"

"That's all right, she's his girl," spoke up a young fellow she recognized as her guide.

"And you?" the other man blurted explosively at Silverstein.

"I'm vit her," he answered truculently.

"She works for him," explained the young fellow. "It's all right, I tell you."

The newcomer grunted and knelt down. He passed a hand over the damp head, grunted again, and arose to his feet.

"This is no case for me," he said. "Send for the ambulance."

Then the thing became a dream to Genevieve. Maybe she had fainted, she did not know, but for what other reason should Silverstein have his arm around her supporting her? All the faces seemed blurred and unreal. Fragments of a discussion came to her ears. The young fellow who had been her guide was saying something about reporters. "You vill get your name in der papers," she could hear Silverstein saying to her, as from a great distance; and she knew she was shaking her head in refusal.

There was an eruption of new faces, and she saw Joe carried out on a canvas stretcher. Silverstein was buttoning the long overcoat and drawing the collar about her face. She felt the night air on her cheek, and looking up saw the clear, cold stars. She jammed into a seat. Silverstein was beside her. Joe was there, too, still on his stretcher, with blankets over his naked body; and there was a man in blue uniform who spoke kindly to her, though she did not know what he said. Horses' hoofs were clattering, and she was lurching somewhere through the night.

Next, light and voices, and a smell of iodoform. This

must be the receiving hospital, she thought, this the operating table, those the doctors. They were examining Joe. One of them, a dark-eyed, dark-bearded, foreign-looking man, rose up from bending over the table.

"Never saw anything like it," he was saying to another man. "The whole back of the skull."

Her lips were hot and dry, and there was an intolerable ache in her throat. But why didn't she cry? She ought to cry; she felt it incumbent upon her. There was Lottie (there had been another change in the dream), across the little narrow cot from her, and she was crying. Somebody was saying something about the coma of death. It was not the foreign-looking doctor, but somebody else. It did not matter who it was. What time was it? As if in answer, she saw the faint white light of dawn on the windows.

"I was going to be married to-day," she said to Lottie.

And from across the cot his sister wailed, "Don't, don't!" and, covering her face, sobbed afresh.

This, then, was the end of it all—of the carpets, and furniture, and the little rented house; of the meetings and walking out, the thrilling nights of starshine, the deliciousness of surrender, the loving and the being loved. She was stunned by the awful facts of this Game she did not understand—the grip it laid on men's souls, its irony and faithlessness, its risks and hazards and fierce insurgences of the blood, making woman pitiful, not the be-all and end-all of man, but his toy and his pastime; to woman his mothering and caretaking, his moods and his moments, but to the Game his days and nights of striving, the tribute of his head and hand, his most patient toil and wildest effort, all the strain and the stress of his being—to the Game, his heart's desire.

Silverstein was helping her to her feet. She obeyed blindly, the daze of the dream still on her. His hand grasped her arm and he was turning her toward the door.

"Oh, why don't you kiss him?" Lottie cried out, her dark eyes mournful and passionate.

Genevieve stooped obediently over the quiet clay and pressed her lips to the lips yet warm. The door opened and she passed into another room. There stood Mrs. Silverstein, with angry eyes that snapped vindictively at sight of her boy's clothes.

Silverstein looked beseechingly at his spouse, but she burst forth savagely:

"Vot did I tell you, eh? Vot did I tell you? You vood haf a bruiser for your steady! An' now your name vill be in all der papers! At a prize fight—vit boy's clothes on! You liddle strumpet! You hussy! You—"

But a flood of tears welled into her eyes and voice, and with her fat arms outstretched, ungainly, ludicrous, holy with motherhood, she tottered over to the quiet girl and folded her to her breast. She muttered gasping, inarticulate love-words, rocking slowly to and fro the while, and patting Genevieve's shoulder with her ponderous hand.

A Piece of Steak

A Piece of Steak

WITH THE LAST MORSEL of bread Tom King wiped his plate clean of the last particle of flour gravy and chewed the resulting mouthful in a slow and meditative way. When he arose from the table, he was oppressed by the feeling that he was distinctly hungry. Yet he alone had eaten. The two children in the other room had been sent early to bed in order that in sleep they might forget they had gone supperless. His wife had touched nothing, and had sat silently and watched him with solicitous eyes. She was a thin, worn woman of the working-class, though signs of an earlier prettiness were not wanting in her face. The flour for the gravy she had borrowed from the neighbour across the hall. The last two ha'pennies had gone to buy the bread.

He sat down by the window on a rickety chair that protested under his weight, and quite mechanically he put his pipe in his mouth and dipped into the side pocket of his coat. The absence of any tobacco made him aware of his action, and, with a scowl for his forgetfulness, he put the pipe away. His movements were slow, almost hulking, as though he were burdened by the heavy weight of his muscles. He was a solid-bodied, stolid-looking man, and his appearance did not suffer from being overprepossessing. His rough clothes were old and slouchy. The uppers of his shoes were too weak to carry the heavy re-soling that was itself of no recent date. And his cotton shirt, a cheap, two shilling affair, showed a frayed collar and ineradicable paint stains.

But it was Tom King's face that advertised him unmistakably for what he was. It was the face of a typical prize-fighter; of one who had put in long years of service in the squared ring and, by that means, developed and emphasized all the marks of the fighting beast. It was distinctly a lowering countenance, and, that no feature of it might escape notice, it was clean-shaven. The lips were shapeless and constituted a mouth harsh to excess, that was like a gash in his face. The jaw was aggressive, brutal, heavy. The eyes, slow of movement and heavy-lidded, were almost expressionless under the shaggy, indrawn brows. Sheer animal that he was, the eyes were the most animal-like feature about him. They were sleepy, lion-like—the eyes of a fighting animal. The forehead slanted quickly back to the hair, which, clipped close, showed every bump of a villainous-looking head. A nose twice broken and moulded variously by countless blows, and a cauliflower ear, permanently swollen and distorted to twice its size, completed his adornment, while the beard, fresh-shaven as it was, sprouted in the skin and gave the face a blue-black stain.

Altogether, it was the face of a man to be afraid of in a dark alley or lonely place. And yet Tom King was not a criminal, nor had he ever done anything criminal. Outside of brawls, common to his walk in life, he had harmed no one. Nor had he ever been known to pick a quarrel. He was a professional, and all the fighting brutishness of him was reserved for his professional appearances. Outside the ring he was slow-going, easy-natured, and, in his younger days, when money was flush, too open-handed for his own good. He bore no grudges and had few enemies. Fighting was a business with him. In the ring he struck to hurt, struck to maim, struck to destroy; but there was no animus in it. It was a plain business proposition. Audiences assembled and paid for the spectacle of men knocking each other out. The winner took the big end of the purse. When Tom King faced the Woolloomoolloo Gouger, twenty years before, he knew that the Gouger's jaw was only four months healed after having been broken in a Newcastle bout. And he had played for that jaw and broken it again in the ninth round, not because he bore the Gouger any ill-will, but because that was the surest way to put the Gouger out and win the big end of the purse. Nor had the Gouger borne him any ill-will for it. It was the game, and both knew the game and played it.

Tom King had never been a talker, and he sat by the window, morosely silent, staring at his hands. The veins stood out on the backs of the hands, large and swollen; and the knuckles, smashed and battered and malformed, testified to the use to which they had been put. He had never heard that a man's life was the life of his arteries, but well he knew the meaning of those big upstanding veins. His heart had pumped too much blood through them at top pressure. They no longer did the work. He had stretched the elasticity out of them, and with their distension had passed his endurance. He tired easily now. No longer could he do a fast twenty rounds, hammer and tongs, fight, fight, fight, from gong to gong, with fierce rally on top of fierce rally, beaten to the ropes and in turn beating his opponent to the ropes, and rallying fiercest and fastest of all in that last, twentieth round, with the house on its feet and yelling, himself rushing, striking, ducking, raining showers of blows upon showers of blows and receiving showers of blows in return, and all the time the heart faithfully pumping the surging blood through the adequate veins. The veins, swollen at the time, had always shrunk down again, though each time, imperceptibly at first, not quite—remaining just a trifle larger than before. He stared at them and at his battered knuckles, and, for the moment, caught a vision of the youthful excellence of those hands before the first knuckle had been smashed on the head of Benny Jones, otherwise known as the Welsh Terror.

The impression of his hunger came back on him.

"Blimey, but couldn't I go a piece of steak!" he muttered aloud, clenching his huge fists and spitting out a smothered oath.

"I tried both Burke's an' Sawley's," his wife said half apologetically.

"An' they wouldn't?" he demanded.

"Not a ha'penny. Burke said—" She faltered.

"G'wan! Wot'd he say?"

"As how 'e was thinkin' Sandel ud do ye to-night, an' as how yer score was comfortable big as it was."

Tom King grunted, but did not reply. He was busy thinking of the bull terrier he had kept in his younger days to which he had fed steaks without end. Burke would have given him credit for a thousand steaks—then. But times had changed. Tom King was getting old; and old men, fighting before second-rate clubs, couldn't expect to run bills of any size with the tradesmen.

He had got up in the morning with a longing for a piece of steak, and the longing had not abated. He had not had a fair training for this fight. It was a drought year in Australia, times were hard, and even the most irregular work was difficult to find. He had had no sparring partner, and his food had not been of the best nor always sufficient. He had done a few days' navvy work when he could get it, and he had run around the Domain in the early mornings to get his legs in shape. But it was hard, training without a partner and with a wife and two kiddies that must be fed. Credit with the tradesmen had undergone very slight expansion when he was matched with Sandel. The secretary of the Gayety Club had advanced him three pounds—the loser's end of the purse—and beyond that had refused to go. Now and again he had managed to borrow a few shillings from old pals, who would have lent more only that it was a drought year and they were hard put themselves. No—and there was no use in disguising the fact—his training had not been satisfactory. He should have had better food and no worries. Besides, when a man is forty, it is harder to get into condition than when he is twenty.

"What time is it, Lizzie?" he asked.

His wife went across the hall to inquire, and came

back.

"Quarter before eight."

"They'll be startin' the first bout in a few minutes," he said. "Only a try-out. Then there's a four-round spar 'tween Dealer Wells an' Gridley, an' a ten-round go 'tween Starlight an' some sailor bloke. I don't come on for over an hour."

At the end of another silent ten minutes, he rose to his feet.

"Truth is, Lizzie, I ain't had proper trainin'."

He reached for his hat and started for the door. He did not offer to kiss her—he never did on going out—but on this night she dared to kiss him, throwing her arms around him and compelling him to bend down to her face. She looked quite small against the massive bulk of the man.

"Good luck, Tom," she said. "You gotter do 'im."

"Ay, I gotter do 'im," he repeated. "That's all there is to it. I jus' gotter do 'im."

He laughed with an attempt at heartiness, while she pressed more closely against him. Across her shoulders he looked around the bare room. It was all he had in the world, with the rent overdue, and her and the kiddies. And he was leaving it to go out into the night to get meat for his mate and cubs—not like a modern working-man going to his machine grind, but in the old, primitive, royal, animal way, by fighting for it.

"I gotter do 'im," he repeated, this time a hint of desperation in his voice. "If it's a win, it's thirty quid—an' I can pay all that's owin', with a lump o' money left over. If it's a lose, I get naught—not even a penny for me to ride home on the tram. The secretary's give all that's comin' from a loser's end. Good-bye, old woman. I'll come straight home if it's a win."

"An' I'll be waitin' up," she called to him along the hall.

It was full two miles to the Gayety, and as he walked along he remembered how in his palmy days—he had once been the heavyweight champion of New South Wales—he would have ridden in a cab to the fight, and how, most likely, some heavy backer would have paid for the cab and ridden with him. There were Tommy Burns and that Yankee nigger, Jack Johnson—they rode about in motor-cars. And he walked! And, as any man knew, a hard two miles was not the best preliminary to a fight. He was an old un, and the world did not wag well with old uns. He was good for nothing now except navvy work, and his broken nose and swollen ear were against him even in that. He found himself wishing that he had learned a trade. It would have been better in the long run. But no one had told him, and he knew, deep down in his heart, that he would not have listened if they had. It had been so easy. Big money—sharp, glorious fights—periods of rest and loafing in between—a following of eager flatterers, the slaps on the back, the shakes of the hand, the toffs glad to buy him a drink for the privilege of five minutes' talk—and the glory of it, the yelling houses, the whirlwind finish, the referee's "King wins!" and his name in the sporting columns next day.

Those had been times! But he realized now, in his slow, ruminating way, that it was the old uns he had been putting away. He was Youth, rising; and they were Age, sinking. No wonder it had been easy—they with their swollen veins and battered knuckles and weary in the bones of them from the long battles they had already fought. He remembered the time he put out old Stowsher Bill, at Rush-Cutters Bay, in the eighteenth round, and how old Bill had cried afterward in the dressing-room like a baby. Perhaps old Bill's rent had been overdue. Perhaps he'd had at home a missus an' a couple of kiddies. And perhaps Bill, that very day of the fight, had had a hungering for a piece of steak. Bill had fought game and taken incredible punishment. He could see now, after he had gone through the mill himself, that Stowsher Bill had fought for a bigger stake, that night twenty years ago, than had young Tom King, who had fought for glory and easy money. No wonder Stowsher Bill had cried afterward in the dressing-room.

Well, a man had only so many fights in him, to begin with. It was the iron law of the game. One man might have a hundred hard fights in him, another man only twenty; each, according to the make of him and the quality of his fibre, had a definite number, and, when he had fought them, he was done. Yes, he had had more fights in him than most of them, and he had had far more than his share of the hard, gruelling fights—the kind that worked the heart and lungs to bursting, that took the elastic out of the arteries and made hard knots of muscle out of Youth's sleek suppleness, that wore out nerve and stamina and made brain and bones weary from excess of effort and endurance overwrought. Yes, he had done better than all of them. There were none of his old fighting partners left. He was the last of the old guard. He had seen them all finished, and he had had a hand in finishing some of them.

They had tried him out against the old uns, and one after another he had put them away—laughing when, like old Stowsher Bill, they cried in the dressing-room. And now he was an old un, and they tried out the youngsters on him. There was that bloke, Sandel. He had come over from New Zealand with a record behind him. But nobody in Australia knew anything about him, so they put him up against old Tom King. If Sandel made a showing, he would be given better men to fight, with bigger purses to win; so it was to be depended upon that he would put up a fierce battle. He had everything to win by it—money and glory and career; and Tom King was the grizzled old chopping-block that guarded the highway to fame and fortune. And he had nothing to win except thirty quid, to pay to the landlord and the tradesmen. And, as Tom King thus ruminated, there came to his stolid vision the form of Youth, glorious Youth, rising exultant and invincible, supple of muscle and silken of skin, with heart and lungs that had never been tired and torn and that laughed at limitation of effort. Yes, Youth was the Nemesis. It destroyed the old uns and recked not that, in so doing, it destroyed itself. It enlarged its arteries and smashed its knuckles, and was in turn destroyed by Youth. For Youth was ever youthful. It was only Age that grew old.

At Castlereagh Street he turned to the left, and three blocks along came to the Gayety. A crowd of young larrikins hanging outside the door made respectful way for him, and he heard one say to another: "That's 'im! That's Tom King!"

Inside, on the way to his dressing-room, he

encountered the secretary, a keen-eyed, shrewd-faced young man, who shook his hand.

"How are you feelin', Tom?" he asked.

"Fit as a fiddle," King answered, though he knew that he lied, and that if he had a quid, he would give it right there for a good piece of steak.

When he emerged from the dressing-room, his seconds behind him, and came down the aisle to the squared ring in the centre of the hall, a burst of greeting and applause went up from the waiting crowd. He acknowledged salutations right and left, though few of the faces did he know. Most of them were the faces of kiddies unborn when he was winning his first laurels in the squared ring. He leaped lightly to the raised platform and ducked through the ropes to his corner, where he sat down on a folding stool. Jack Ball, the referee, came over and shook his hand. Ball was a broken-down pugilist who for over ten years had not entered the ring as a principal. King was glad that he had him for referee. They were both old uns. If he should rough it with Sandel a bit beyond the rules, he knew Ball could be depended upon to pass it by.

Aspiring young heavyweights, one after another, were climbing into the ring and being presented to the audience by the referee. Also, he issued their challenges for them.

"Young Pronto," Bill announced, "from North Sydney, challenges the winner for fifty pounds side bet."

The audience applauded, and applauded again as Sandel himself sprang through the ropes and sat down in his corner. Tom King looked across the ring at him curiously, for in a few minutes they would be locked together in merciless combat, each trying with all the force of him to knock the other into unconsciousness. But little could he see, for Sandel, like himself, had trousers and sweater on over his ring costume. His face was strongly handsome, crowned with a curly mop of yellow hair, while his thick, muscular neck hinted at bodily magnificence.

Young Pronto went to one corner and then the other, shaking hands with the principals and dropping down out of the ring. The challenges went on. Ever Youth climbed through the ropes—Youth unknown, but insatiable—crying out to mankind that with strength and skill it would match issues with the winner. A few years before, in his own heyday of invincibleness, Tom King would have been amused and bored by these preliminaries. But now he sat fascinated, unable to shake the vision of Youth from his eyes. Always were these youngsters rising up in the boxing game, springing through the ropes and shouting their defiance; and always were the old uns going down before them. They climbed to success over the bodies of the old uns. And ever they came, more and more youngsters—Youth unquenchable and irresistible—and ever they put the old uns away, themselves becoming old uns and travelling the same downward path, while behind them, ever pressing on them, was Youth eternal—the new babies, grown lusty and dragging their elders down, with behind them more babies to the end of time—Youth that must have its will and that will never die.

King glanced over to the press box and nodded to Morgan, of the Sportsman, and Corbett, of the Referee. Then he held out his hands, while Sid Sullivan and Charley Bates, his seconds, slipped on his gloves and laced them tight, closely watched by one of Sandel's seconds, who first examined critically the tapes on King's knuckles. A second of his own was in Sandel's corner, performing a like office. Sandel's trousers were pulled off, and, as he stood up, his sweater was skinned off over his head. And Tom King, looking, saw Youth incarnate, deep-chested, heavy-thewed, with muscles that slipped and slid like live things under the white satin skin. The whole body was a-crawl with life, and Tom King knew that it was a life that had never oozed its freshness out through the aching pores during the long fights wherein Youth paid its toll and departed not quite so young as when it entered.

The two men advanced to meet each other, and, as the gong sounded and the seconds clattered out of the ring with the folding stools, they shook hands and instantly took their fighting attitudes. And instantly, like a mechanism of steel and springs balanced on a hair trigger, Sandel was in and out and in again, landing a left to the eyes, a right to the ribs, ducking a counter, dancing lightly away and dancing menacingly back again. He was swift and clever. It was a dazzling exhibition. The house yelled its approbation. But King was not dazzled. He had fought too many fights and too many youngsters. He knew the blows for what they were—too quick and too deft to be dangerous. Evidently Sandel was going to rush things from the start. It was to be expected. It was the way of Youth, expending its splendour and excellence in wild insurgence and furious onslaught, overwhelming opposition with its own unlimited glory of strength and desire.

Sandel was in and out, here, there, and everywhere, light-footed and eager-hearted, a living wonder of white flesh and stinging muscle that wove itself into a dazzling fabric of attack, slipping and leaping like a flying shuttle from action to action through a thousand actions, all of them centred upon the destruction of Tom King, who stood between him and fortune. And Tom King patiently endured. He knew his business, and he knew Youth now that Youth was no longer his. There was nothing to do till the other lost some of his steam, was his thought, and he grinned to himself as he deliberately ducked so as to receive a heavy blow on the top of his head. It was a wicked thing to do, yet eminently fair according to the rules of the boxing game. A man was supposed to take care of his own knuckles, and, if he insisted on hitting an opponent on the top of the head, he did so at his own peril. King could have ducked lower and let the blow whiz harmlessly past, but he remembered his own early fights and how he smashed his first knuckle on the head of the Welsh Terror. He was but playing the game. That duck had accounted for one of Sandel's knuckles. Not that Sandel would mind it now. He would go on, superbly regardless, hitting as hard as ever throughout the fight. But later on, when the long ring battles had begun to tell, he would regret that knuckle and look back and remember how he smashed it on Tom King's head.

The first round was all Sandel's, and he had the house yelling with the rapidity of his whirlwind rushes. He overwhelmed King with avalanches of punches, and King did nothing. He never struck once, contenting himself with covering up, blocking and ducking and clinching to avoid punishment. He occasionally feinted, shook his head when the weight of a punch landed, and moved stolidly about, never leaping or springing or wasting an ounce of strength. Sandel must foam the froth of Youth away before discreet Age could dare to retaliate. All King's movements were slow and methodical, and his heavy-lidded, slow-moving eyes gave him the appearance of being half asleep or dazed. Yet they were eyes that saw everything, that had been trained to see everything through all his twenty years and odd in the ring. They were eyes that did not blink or waver before an impending blow, but that coolly saw and measured distance.

Seated in his corner for the minute's rest at the end of the round, he lay back with outstretched legs, his arms resting on the right angle of the ropes, his chest and abdomen heaving frankly and deeply as he gulped down the air driven by the towels of his seconds. He listened with closed eyes to the voices of the house, "Why don't yeh fight, Tom?" many were crying. "Yeh ain't afraid of 'im, are yeh?"

"Muscle-bound," he heard a man on a front seat comment. "He can't move quicker. Two to one on Sandel, in quids."

The gong struck and the two men advanced from their corners. Sandel came forward fully three-quarters of the distance, eager to begin again; but King was content to advance the shorter distance. It was in line with his policy of economy. He had not been well trained, and he had not had enough to eat, and every step counted. Besides, he had already walked two miles to the ringside. It was a repetition of the first round, with Sandel attacking like a whirlwind and with the audience indignantly demanding why King did not fight. Beyond feinting and several slowly delivered and ineffectual blows he did nothing save block and stall and clinch. Sandel wanted to make the pace fast, while King, out of his wisdom, refused to accommodate him. He grinned with a certain wistful pathos in his ring-battered countenance, and went on cherishing his strength with the jealousy of which only Age is capable. Sandel was Youth, and he threw his strength away with the munificent abandon of Youth. To King belonged the ring generalship, the wisdom bred of long, aching fights. He watched with cool eyes and head, moving slowly and waiting for Sandel's froth to foam away. To the majority of the onlookers it seemed as though King was hopelessly outclassed, and they voiced their opinion in offers of three to one on Sandel. But there were wise ones, a few, who knew King of old time, and who covered what they considered easy money.

The third round began as usual, one-sided, with Sandel doing all the leading, and delivering all the punishment. A half-minute had passed when Sandel, over-confident, left an opening. King's eyes and right arm flashed in the same instant. It was his first real blow—a hook, with the twisted arch of the arm to make it rigid, and with all the weight of the half-pivoted body behind it. It was like a sleepy-seeming lion suddenly thrusting out a lightning paw. Sandel, caught on the side of the jaw, was felled like a bullock. The audience gasped and murmured awe-stricken applause. The man was not muscle-bound, after all, and he could drive a blow like a trip-hammer.

Sandel was shaken. He rolled over and attempted to

rise, but the sharp yells from his seconds to take the count restrained him. He knelt on one knee, ready to rise, and waited, while the referee stood over him, counting the seconds loudly in his ear. At the ninth he rose in fighting attitude, and Tom King, facing him, knew regret that the blow had not been an inch nearer the point of the jaw. That would have been a knock-out, and he could have carried the thirty quid home to the missus and the kiddies.

The round continued to the end of its three minutes, Sandel for the first time respectful of his opponent and King slow of movement and sleepy-eyed as ever. As the round neared its close, King, warned of the fact by sight of the seconds crouching outside ready for the spring in through the ropes, worked the fight around to his own corner. And when the gong struck, he sat down immediately on the waiting stool, while Sandel had to walk all the way across the diagonal of the square to his own corner. It was a little thing, but it was the sum of little things that counted. Sandel was compelled to walk that many more steps, to give up that much energy, and to lose a part of the precious minute of rest. At the beginning of every round King loafed slowly out from his corner, forcing his opponent to advance the greater distance. The end of every round found the fight manoeuvred by King into his own corner so that he could immediately sit down.

Two more rounds went by, in which King was parsimonious of effort and Sandel prodigal. The latter's attempt to force a fast pace made King uncomfortable, for a fair percentage of the multitudinous blows showered upon him went home. Yet King persisted in his dogged slowness, despite the crying of the young hot-heads for him to go in and fight. Again, in the sixth round, Sandel was careless, again Tom King's fearful right flashed out to the jaw, and again Sandel took the nine seconds count.

By the seventh round Sandel's pink of condition was gone, and he settled down to what he knew was to be the hardest fight in his experience. Tom King was an old un, but a better old un than he had ever encountered—an old un who never lost his head, who was remarkably able at defence, whose blows had the impact of a knotted club, and who had a knockout in either hand. Nevertheless, Tom King dared not hit often. He never forgot his battered knuckles, and knew that every hit must count if the knuckles were to last out the fight. As he sat in his corner, glancing across at his opponent, the thought came to him that the sum of his wisdom and Sandel's youth would constitute a world's champion heavyweight. But that was the trouble. Sandel would never become a world champion. He lacked the wisdom, and the only way for him to get it was to buy it with Youth; and when wisdom was his, Youth would have been spent in buying it.

King took every advantage he knew. He never missed an opportunity to clinch, and in effecting most of the clinches his shoulder drove stiffly into the other's ribs. In the philosophy of the ring a shoulder was as good as a punch so far as damage was concerned, and a great deal better so far as concerned expenditure of effort. Also, in the clinches King rested his weight on his opponent, and was loath to let go. This compelled the interference of the referee, who tore them apart, always assisted by Sandel, who had not yet learned to rest. He could not refrain from using those glorious flying arms and writhing muscles of his, and when the other rushed into a clinch, striking shoulder against ribs, and with head resting under Sandel's left arm, Sandel almost invariably swung his right behind his own back and into the projecting face. It was a clever stroke, much admired by the audience, but it was not dangerous, and was, therefore, just that much wasted strength. But Sandel was tireless and unaware of limitations, and King grinned and doggedly endured.

Sandel developed a fierce right to the body, which made it appear that King was taking an enormous amount of punishment, and it was only the old ringsters who appreciated the deft touch of King's left glove to the other's biceps just before the impact of the blow. It was true, the blow landed each time; but each time it was robbed of its power by that touch on the biceps. In the ninth round, three times inside a minute, King's right hooked its twisted arch to the jaw; and three times Sandel's body, heavy as it was, was levelled to the mat. Each time he took the nine seconds allowed him and rose to his feet, shaken and jarred, but still strong. He had lost much of his speed, and he wasted less effort. He was fighting grimly; but he continued to draw upon his chief asset, which was Youth. King's chief asset was experience. As his vitality had dimmed and his vigour abated, he had replaced them with cunning, with wisdom born of the long fights and with a careful shepherding of strength. Not alone had he learned never to make a superfluous movement, but he had learned how to seduce an opponent into throwing his strength away. Again and again, by feint of foot and hand and body he continued to inveigle Sandel into leaping back, ducking, or countering. King rested, but he never permitted Sandel to rest. It was the strategy of Age.

Early in the tenth round King began stopping the other's rushes with straight lefts to the face, and Sandel, grown wary, responded by drawing the left, then by ducking it and delivering his right in a swinging hook to the side of the head. It was too high up to be vitally effective; but when first it landed, King knew the old, familiar descent of the black veil of unconsciousness across his mind. For the instant, or for the slighest fraction of an instant, rather, he ceased. In the one moment he saw his opponent ducking out of his field of vision and the background of white, watching faces; in the next moment he again saw his opponent and the background of faces. It was as if he had slept for a time and just opened his eyes again, and yet the interval of unconsciousness was so microscopically short that there had been no time for him to fall. The audience saw him totter and his knees give, and then saw him recover and tuck his chin deeper into the shelter of his left shoulder.

Several times Sandel repeated the blow, keeping King partially dazed, and then the latter worked out his defence, which was also a counter. Feinting with his left he took a half-step backward, at the same time upper cutting with the whole strength of his right. So accurately was it timed that it landed squarely on Sandel's face in the full, downward sweep of the duck, and Sandel lifted in the air and curled backward, striking the mat on his head and shoulders. Twice King achieved this, then turned loose and hammered his opponent to the ropes. He gave Sandel no chance to rest or to set himself, but smashed blow in upon blow till the house rose to its feet and the air was filled with an unbroken roar of applause. But Sandel's strength and endurance were superb, and he continued to stay on his feet. A knock-out seemed certain, and a captain of police, appalled at the dreadful punishment, arose by the ringside to stop the fight. The gong struck for the end of the round and Sandel staggered to his corner, protesting to the captain that he was sound and strong. To prove it, he threw two back-air-springs, and the police captain gave in.

Tom King, leaning back in his corner and breathing hard, was disappointed. If the fight had been stopped, the referee, perforce, would have rendered him the decision and the purse would have been his. Unlike Sandel, he was not fighting for glory or career, but for thirty quid. And now Sandel would recuperate in the minute of rest.

Youth will be served—this saying flashed into King's mind, and he remembered the first time he had heard it, the night when he had put away Stowsher Bill. The toff who had bought him a drink after the fight and patted him on the shoulder had used those words. Youth will be served! The toff was right. And on that night in the long ago he had been Youth. To-night Youth sat in the opposite corner. As for himself, he had been fighting for half an hour now, and he was an old man. Had he fought like Sandel, he would not have lasted fifteen minutes. But the point was that he did not recuperate. Those upstanding arteries and that sorely tried heart would not enable him to gather strength in the intervals between the rounds. And he had not had sufficient strength in him to begin with. His legs were heavy under him and beginning to cramp. He should not have walked those two miles to the fight. And there was the steak which he had got up longing for that morning. A great and terrible hatred rose up in him for the butchers who had refused him credit. It was hard for an old man to go into a fight without enough to eat. And a piece of steak was such a little thing, a few pennies at best; yet it meant thirty quid to him.

With the gong that opened the eleventh round, Sandel rushed, making a show of freshness which he did not really possess. King knew it for what it was—a bluff as old as the game itself. He clinched to save himself, then, going free, allowed Sandel to get set. This was what King desired. He feinted with his left, drew the answering duck and swinging upward hook, then made the half-step backward, delivered the upper cut full to the face and crumpled Sandel over to the mat. After that he never let him rest, receiving punishment himself, but inflicting far more, smashing Sandel to the ropes, hooking and driving all manner of blows into him, tearing away from his clinches or punching him out of attempted clinches, and ever when Sandel would have fallen, catching him with one uplifting hand and with the other immediately smashing him into the ropes where he could not fall.

The house by this time had gone mad, and it was his house, nearly every voice yelling: "Go it, Tom!" "Get 'im! Get 'im!" "You've got 'im, Tom! You've got 'im!" It was to be a whirlwind finish, and that was what a ringside audience paid to see.

And Tom King, who for half an hour had conserved

his strength, now expended it prodigally in the one great effort he knew he had in him. It was his one chance—now or not at all. His strength was waning fast, and his hope was that before the last of it ebbed out of him he would have beaten his opponent down for the count. And as he continued to strike and force, coolly estimating the weight of his blows and the quality of the damage wrought, he realized how hard a man Sandel was to knock out. Stamina and endurance were his to an extreme degree, and they were the virgin stamina and endurance of Youth. Sandel was certainly a coming man. He had it in him. Only out of such rugged fibre were successful fighters fashioned.

Sandel was reeling and staggering, but Tom King's legs were cramping and his knuckles going back on him. Yet he steeled himself to strike the fierce blows, every one of which brought anguish to his tortured hands. Though now he was receiving practically no punishment, he was weakening as rapidly as the other. His blows went home, but there was no longer the weight behind them, and each blow was the result of a severe effort of will. His legs were like lead, and they dragged visibly under him; while Sandel's backers, cheered by this symptom, began calling encouragement to their man.

King was spurred to a burst of effort. He delivered two blows in succession—a left, a trifle too high, to the solar plexus, and a right cross to the jaw. They were not heavy blows, yet so weak and dazed was Sandel that he went down and lay quivering. The referee stood over him, shouting the count of the fatal seconds in his ear. If before the tenth second was called, he did not rise, the fight was lost. The house stood in hushed silence. King rested on trembling legs. A mortal dizziness was upon him, and before his eyes the sea of faces sagged and swayed, while to his ears, as from a remote distance, came the count of the referee. Yet he looked upon the fight as his. It was impossible that a man so punished could rise.

Only Youth could rise, and Sandel rose. At the fourth second he rolled over on his face and groped blindly for the ropes. By the seventh second he had dragged himself to his knee, where he rested, his head rolling groggily on his shoulders. As the referee cried "Nine!" Sandel stood upright, in proper stalling position, his left arm wrapped about his face, his right wrapped about his stomach. Thus were his vital points guarded, while he lurched forward toward King in the hope of effecting a clinch and gaining more time.

At the instant Sandel arose, King was at him, but the two blows he delivered were muffled on the stalled arms. The next moment Sandel was in the clinch and holding on desperately while the referee strove to drag the two men apart. King helped to force himself free. He knew the rapidity with which Youth recovered, and he knew that Sandel was his if he could prevent that recovery. One stiff punch would do it. Sandel was his, indubitably his. He had out-generalled him, out-fought him, out-pointed him. Sandel reeled out of the clinch, balanced on the hair line between defeat or survival. One good blow would topple him over and down and out. And Tom King, in a flash of bitterness, remembered the piece of steak and wished that he had it then behind that necessary punch he must deliver. He nerved himself for the blow, but it was not heavy enough nor swift enough. Sandel swayed, but did not fall, staggering back to the ropes and holding on. King staggered after him, and, with a pang like that of dissolution, delivered another blow. But his body had deserted him. All that was left of him was a fighting intelligence that was dimmed and clouded from exhaustion. The blow that was aimed for the jaw struck no higher than the shoulder. He had willed the blow higher, but the tired muscles had not been able to obey. And, from the impact of the blow, Tom King himself reeled back and nearly fell. Once again he strove. This time his punch missed altogether, and, from absolute weakness, he fell against Sandel and clinched, holding on to him to save himself from sinking to the floor.

King did not attempt to free himself. He had shot his bolt. He was gone. And Youth had been served. Even in the clinch he could feel Sandel growing stronger against him. When the referee thrust them apart, there, before his eyes, he saw Youth recuperate. From instant to instant Sandel grew stronger. His punches, weak and futile at first, became stiff and accurate. Tom King's bleared eyes saw the gloved fist driving at his jaw, and he willed to guard it by interposing his arm. He saw the danger, willed the act; but the arm was too heavy. It seemed burdened with a hundredweight of lead. It would not lift itself, and he strove to lift it with his soul. Then the gloved fist landed home. He experienced a sharp snap that was like an electric spark, and, simultaneously, the veil of blackness enveloped him.

When he opened his eyes again he was in his corner, and he heard the yelling of the audience like the roar of the surf at Bondi Beach. A wet sponge was being pressed against the base of his brain, and Sid Sullivan was blowing cold water in a refreshing spray over his face and chest. His gloves had already been removed, and Sandel, bending over him, was shaking his hand. He bore no ill-will toward the man who had put him out and he returned the grip with a heartiness that made his battered knuckles protest. Then Sandel stepped to the centre of the ring and the audience hushed its pandemonium to hear him accept young Pronto's challenge and offer to increase the side bet to one hundred pounds. King looked on apathetically while his seconds mopped the streaming water from him, dried his face, and prepared him to leave the ring. He felt hungry. It was not the ordinary, gnawing kind, but a great faintness, a palpitation at the pit of the stomach that communicated itself to all his body. He remembered back into the fight to the moment when he had Sandel swaying and tottering on the hair-line balance of defeat. Ah, that piece of steak would have done it! He had lacked just that for the decisive blow, and he had lost. It was all because of the piece of steak.

His seconds were half-supporting him as they helped him through the ropes. He tore free from them, ducked through the ropes unaided, and leaped heavily to the floor, following on their heels as they forced a passage for him down the crowded centre aisle. Leaving the dressing-room for the street, in the entrance to the hall, some young fellow spoke to him.

"W'y didn't yuh go in an' get 'im when yuh 'ad 'im?" the young fellow asked.

"Aw, go to hell!" said Tom King, and passed down the steps to the sidewalk.

The doors of the public-house at the corner were swinging wide, and he saw the lights and the smiling barmaids, heard the many voices discussing the fight and the prosperous chink of money on the bar. Somebody called to him to have a drink. He hesitated perceptibly, then refused and went on his way.

He had not a copper in his pocket, and the two-mile walk home seemed very long. He was certainly getting old. Crossing the Domain, he sat down suddenly on a bench, unnerved by the thought of the missus sitting up for him, waiting to learn the outcome of the fight. That was harder than any knockout, and it seemed almost impossible to face.

He felt weak and sore, and the pain of his smashed knuckles warned him that, even if he could find a job at navvy work, it would be a week before he could grip a pick handle or a shovel. The hunger palpitation at the pit of the stomach was sickening. His wretchedness overwhelmed him, and into his eyes came an unwonted moisture. He covered his face with his hands, and, as he cried, he remembered Stowsher Bill and how he had served him that night in the long ago. Poor old Stowsher Bill! He could understand now why Bill had cried in the dressing-room.

THE MEXICAN

Chapter 1

NOBODY knew his history—they of the Junta least of all. He was their "little mystery," their "big patriot," and in his way he worked as hard for the coming Mexican Revolution as did they. They were tardy in recognizing this, for not one of the Junta liked him. The day he first drifted into their crowded, busy rooms, they all suspected him of being a spy—one of the bought tools of the Diaz secret service. Too many of the comrades were in civil an military prisons scattered over the United States, and others of them, in irons, were even then being taken across the border to be lined up against adobe walls and shot.

At the first sight the boy did not impress them favorably. Boy he was, not more than eighteen and not over large for his years. He announced that he was Felipe Rivera, and that it was his wish to work for the Revolution. That was all—not a wasted word, no further explanation. He stood waiting. There was no smile on his lips, no geniality in his eyes. Big dashing Paulino Vera felt an inward shudder. Here was something forbidding, terrible, inscrutable. There was something venomous and snakelike in the boy's black eyes. They burned like cold fire, as with a vast, concentrated bitterness. He flashed them from the faces of the conspirators to the typewriter which little Mrs. Sethby was industriously operating. His eyes rested on hers but an instant—she had chanced to look up—and she, too, sensed the nameless something that made her pause. She was compelled to read back in order to regain the swing of the letter she was writing.

Paulino Vera looked questioningly at Arrellano and Ramos, and questioningly they looked back and to each other. The indecision of doubt brooded in their eyes. This slender boy was the Unknown, vested with all the menace of the Unknown. He was unrecognizable, something quite beyond the ken of honest, ordinary revolutionists whose fiercest hatred for Diaz and his tyranny after all was only that of honest and ordinary patriots. Here was something else, they knew not what. But Vera, always the most impulsive, the quickest to act, stepped into the breach.

"Very well," he said coldly. "You say you want to work for the Revolution. Take off your coat. Hang it over there. I will show you, come—where are the buckets and cloths. The floor is dirty. You will begin by scrubbing it, and by scrubbing the floors of the other rooms. The spittoons need to be cleaned. Then there are the windows."

"Is it for the Revolution?" the boy asked.

"It is for the Revolution," Vera answered.

Rivera looked cold suspicion at all of them, then proceeded to take off his coat.

"It is well," he said.

And nothing more. Day after day he came to his work—sweeping, scrubbing, cleaning. He emptied the ashes from the stoves, brought up the coal and kindling, and lighted the fires before the most energetic one of them was at his desk.

"Can I sleep here?" he asked once.

Ah, ha! So that was it—the hand of Diaz showing through! To sleep in the rooms of the Junta meant access to their secrets, to the lists of names, to the addresses of comrades down on Mexican soil. The request was denied, and Rivera never spoke of it again. He slept they knew not where, and ate they knew not where nor how. Once, Arrellano offered him a couple of dollars. Rivera declined the money with a shake of the head. When Vera joined in and tried to press it upon him, he said:

"I am working for the Revolution."

It takes money to raise a modern revolution, and always the Junta was pressed. The members starved and toiled, and the longest day was none too long, and yet there were times when it appeared as if the Revolution stood or fell on no more than the matter of a few dollars. Once, the first time, when the rent of the house was two months behind and the landlord was threatening dispossession, it was Felipe Rivera, the scrub-boy in the poor, cheap clothes, worn and threadbare, who laid sixty dollars in gold on May Sethby's desk. There were other times. Three hundred letters, clicked out on the busy typewriters (appeals for assistance, for sanctions from the organized labor groups, requests for square news deals to the editors of newspapers, protests against the high-handed treatment of revolutionists by the United States courts), lay unmailed, awaiting postage. Vera's watch had disappeared—the old-fashioned gold repeater that had been his father's. Likewise had gone the plain gold band from May Setbby's third finger. Things were desperate. Ramos and Arrellano pulled their long mustaches in despair. The letters must go off, and the Post Office allowed no credit to purchasers of stamps. Then it was that Rivera put on his hat and went out. When he came back he laid a thousand two-cent stamps on May Sethby's desk.

"I wonder if it is the cursed gold of Diaz?" said Vera to the comrades.

They elevated their brows and could not decide. And Felipe Rivera, the scrubber for the Revolution, continued, as occasion arose, to lay down gold and silver for the Junta's use.

And still they could not bring themselves to like him. They did not know him. His ways were not theirs. He gave no confidences. He repelled all probing. Youth that he was, they could never nerve themselves to dare to question him.

"A great and lonely spirit, perhaps, I do not know, I do not know," Arrellano said helplessly.

"He is not human," said Ramos.

"His soul has been seared," said May Sethby. "Light and laughter have been burned out of him. He is like one dead, and yet he is fearfully alive."

"He has been through hell," said Vera. "No man could look like that who has not been through hell—and he is only a boy."

Yet they could not like him. He never talked, never inquired, never suggested. He would stand listening, expressionless, a thing dead, save for his eyes, coldly burning, while their talk of the Revolution ran high and warm. From face to face and speaker to speaker his eyes would turn, boring like gimlets of incandescent ice, disconcerting and perturbing.

"He is no spy," Vera confided to May Sethby. "He is a patriot—mark me, the greatest patriot of us all. I know it, I feel it, here in my heart and head I feel it. But him I know not at all."

"He has a bad temper," said May Sethby.

"I know," said Vera, with a shudder. "He has looked at me with those eyes of his. They do not love; they threaten; they are savage as a wild tiger's. I know, if I should prove unfaithful to the Cause, that he would kill me. He has no heart. He is pitiless as steel, keen and cold as frost. He is like moonshine in a winter night when a man freezes to death on some lonely mountain top. I am not afraid of Diaz and all his killers; but this boy, of him am I afraid. I tell you true. I am afraid. He is the breath of death."

Yet Vera it was who persuaded the others to give the first trust to Rivera. The line of communication between Los Angeles and Lower California had broken down. Three of the comrades had dug their own graves and been shot into them. Two more were United States prisoners in Los Angeles. Juan Alvarado, the Federal commander, was a monster. All their plans did he checkmate. They could no longer gain access to the active revolutionists, and the incipient ones, in Lower California.

Young Rivera was given his instructions and dispatched south. When he returned, the line of communication was reestablished, and Juan Alvarado was dead. He had been found in bed, a knife hilt-deep in his breast. This had exceeded Rivera's instructions, but they of the Junta knew the times of his movements. They did not ask him. He said nothing. But they looked at one another and conjectured.

"I have told you," said Vera. "Diaz has more to fear from this youth than from any man. He is implacable. He is the hand of God."

The bad temper, mentioned by May Sethby, and sensed by them all, was evidenced by physical proofs. Now he appeared with a cut lip, a blackened cheek, or a swollen ear. It was patent that he brawled, somewhere in that outside world where he ate and slept, gained money, and moved in ways unknown to them. As the time passed, he had come to set type for the little revolutionary sheet they published weekly. There were occasions when he was unable to set type, when his knuckles were bruised and battered, when his thumbs were injured and helpless, when one arm or the other hung wearily at his side while his face was drawn with unspoken pain.

"A wastrel," said Arrellano.

"A frequenter of low places," said Ramos.

"But where does he get the money?" Vera demanded. "Only to-day, just now, have I learned that he paid the bill for white paper—one hundred and forty dollars."

"There are his absences," said May Sethby. "He never explains them."

"We should set a spy upon him," Ramos propounded.

"I should not care to be that spy," said Vera. "I fear you would never see me again, save to bury me. He has a terrible passion. Not even God would he permit to stand between him and the way of his passion."

"I feel like a child before him," Ramos confessed.

"To me he is power—he is the primitive, the wild wolf, the striking rattlesnake, the stinging centipede," said Arrellano.

"He is the Revolution incarnate," said Vera. "He is the flame and the spirit of it, the insatiable cry for vengeance that makes no cry but that slays noiselessly. He is a destroying angel in moving through the still watches of the night."

"I could weep over him," said May Sethby. "He knows nobody. He hates all people. Us he tolerates, for we are the way of his desire. He is alone.... lonely." Her voice broke in a half sob and there was dimness in her eyes.

Rivera's ways and times were truly mysterious. There were periods when they did not see him for a week at a time. Once, he was away a month. These occasions were always capped by his return, when, without advertisement or speech, he laid gold coins on May Sethby's desk. Again, for days and weeks, he spent all his time with the Junta. And yet again, for irregular periods, he would disappear through the heart of each day, from early morning until late afternoon. At such times he came early and remained late. Arrellano had found him at midnight, setting type with fresh swollen knuckles, or mayhap it was his lip, new-split, that still bled.

CHAPTER 2

THE TIME OF THE CRISIS approached. Whether or not the Revolution would be depended upon the Junta, and the Junta was hard-pressed. The need for money was greater than ever before, while money was harder to get. Patriots had given their last cent and now could give no more. Section gang laborers-fugitive peons from Mexico—were contributing half their scanty wages. But more than that was needed. The heart-breaking, conspiring, undermining toil of years approached fruition. The time was ripe. The Revolution hung on the balance. One shove more, one last heroic effort, and it would tremble across the scales to victory. They knew their Mexico. Once started, the Revolution would take care of itself. The whole Diaz machine would go down like a house of cards. The border was ready to rise. One Yankee, with a hundred I.W.W. men, waited the word to cross over the border and begin the conquest of Lower California. But he needed guns. And clear across to the Atlantic, the Junta in touch with them all and all of them needing guns, mere adventurers, soldiers of fortune, bandits, disgruntled American union men, socialists, anarchists, rough-necks, Mexican exiles, peons escaped from bondage, whipped miners from the bull-pens of Coeur d'Alene and Colorado who desired only the more vindictively to fight—all the flotsam and jetsam of wild spirits from the madly complicated modern world. And it was guns and ammunition, ammunition and guns—the unceasing and eternal cry.

Fling this heterogeneous, bankrupt, vindictive mass across the border, and the Revolution was on. The custom house, the northern ports of entry, would be captured. Diaz could not resist. He dared not throw the weight of his armies against them, for he must hold the south. And through the south the flame would spread despite. The people would rise. The defenses of city after city would crumple up. State after state would totter down. And at last, from every side, the victorious armies of the Revolution would close in on the City of Mexico itself, Diaz's last stronghold.

But the money. They had the men, impatient and urgent, who would use the guns. They knew the traders who would sell and deliver the guns. But to culture the Revolution thus far had exhausted the Junta. The last dollar had been spent, the last resource and the last starving patriot milked dry, and the great adventure still trembled on the scales. Guns and ammunition! The ragged battalions must be armed. But how? Ramos lamented his confiscated estates. Arrellano wailed the spendthriftness of his youth. May Sethby wondered if it would have been different had they of the Junta been more economical in the past.

"To think that the freedom of Mexico should stand or fall on a few paltry thousands of dollars," said Paulino Vera.

Despair was in all their faces. Jose Amarillo, their last hope, a recent convert, who had promised money, had been apprehended at his hacienda in Chihuahua and shot against his own stable wall. The news had just come through.

Rivera, on his knees, scrubbing, looked up, with suspended brush, his bare arms flecked with soapy, dirty water.

"Will five thousand do it?" he asked.

They looked their amazement. Vera nodded and swallowed. He could not speak, but he was on the instant invested with a vast faith.

"Order the guns," Rivera said, and thereupon was guilty of the longest flow of words they had ever heard him utter. "The time is short. In three weeks I shall bring you the five thousand. It is well. The weather will be warmer for those who fight. Also, it is the best I can do."

Vera fought his faith. It was incredible. Too many fond hopes had been shattered since he had begun to play the revolution game. He believed this threadbare scrubber of the Revolution, and yet he dared not believe.

"You are crazy," he said.

"In three weeks," said Rivera. "Order the guns."

He got up, rolled down his sleeves, and put on his coat.

"Order the guns," he said.

"I am going now."

CHAPTER 3

AFTER HURRYING AND SCURRING, much telephoning and bad language, a night session was held in Kelly's office. Kelly was rushed with business; also, he was unlucky. He had brought Danny Ward out from New York, arranged the fight for him with Billy Carthey, the date was three weeks away, and for two days now, carefully concealed from the sporting writers, Carthey had been lying up, badly injured. There was no one to take his place. Kelly had been burning the wires East to every eligible lightweight, but they were tied up with dates and contracts. And now hope had revived, though faintly.

"You've got a hell of a nerve," Kelly addressed Rivera, after one look, as soon as they got together.

Hate that was malignant was in Rivera's eyes, but his face remained impassive.

"I can lick Ward," was all he said.

"How do you know? Ever see him fight?"

Rivera shook his head.

"He can beat you up with one hand and both eyes

closed."

Rivera shrugged his shoulders.

"Haven't you got anything to say?" the fight promoter snarled.

"I can lick him."

"Who'd you ever fight, anyway!" Michael Kelly demanded. Michael was the promotor's brother, and ran the Yellowstone pool rooms where he made goodly sums on the fight game.

Rivera favored him with a bitter, unanswering stare.

The promoter's secretary, a distinctively sporty young man, sneered audibly.

"Well, you know Roberts," Kelly broke the hostile silence. "He ought to be here. I've sent for him. Sit down and wait, though f rom the looks of you, you haven't got a chance. I can't throw the public down with a bum fight. Ringside seats are selling at fifteen dollars, you know that."

When Roberts arrived, it was patent that he was mildly drunk. He was a tall, lean, slack-jointed individual, and his walk, like his talk, was a smooth and languid drawl.

Kelly went straight to the point.

"Look here, Roberts, you've been bragging you discovered this little Mexican. You know Carthey's broke his arm. Well, this little yellow streak has the gall to blow in to-day and say he'll take Carthey's place. What about it?"

"It's all right, Kelly," came the slow response. "He can put up a fight."

"I suppose you'll be sayin' next that he can lick Ward," Kelly snapped.

Roberts considered judicially.

"No, I won't say that. Ward's a top-notcher and a ring general. But he can't hashhouse Rivera in short order. I know Rivera. Nobody can get his goat. He ain't got a goat that I could ever discover. And he's a two-handed fighter. He can throw in the sleep-makers from any position."

"Never mind that. What kind of a show can he put up? You've been conditioning and training fighters all your life. I take off my hat to your judgment. Can he give the public a run for its money?"

"He sure can, and he'll worry Ward a mighty heap on top of it. You don't know that boy. I do. I discovered him. He ain't got a goat. He's a devil. He's a wizzy-wooz if anybody should ask you. He'll make Ward sit up with a show of local talent that'll make the rest of you sit up. I won't say he'll lick Ward, but he'll put up such a show that you'll all know he's a comer."

"All right." Kelly turned to his secretary. "Ring up Ward. I warned him to show up if I thought it worth while. He's right across at the Yellowstone, throwin' chests and doing the popular."

Kelly turned back to the conditioner. "Have a drink?"

Roberts sipped his highball and unburdened himself.

"Never told you how I discovered the little cuss. It was a couple of years ago he showed up out at the quarters. I was getting Prayne ready for his fight with Delaney. Prayne's wicked. He ain't got a tickle of mercy in his make-up. I chopped up his pardner's something cruel, and I couldn't find a willing boy that'd work with him. I'd noticed this little starved Mexican kid hanging around, and I was desperate. So I grabbed him, shoved on the gloves and put him in. He was tougher'n rawhide, but weak. And he didn't know the first letter in the alphabet of boxing. Prayne chopped him to ribbons. But he hung on for two sickening rounds, when he fainted. Starvation, that was all. Battered! You couldn't have recognized him. I gave him half a dollar and a square meal. You oughta seen him wolf it down. He hadn't had the end of a bite for a couple of days. That's the end of him, thinks I. But next day he showed up, stiff an' sore, ready for another half and a square meal. And he done better as time went by. Just a born fighter, and tough beyond belief. He hasn't a heart. He's a piece of ice. And he never talked eleven words in a string since I know him. He saws wood and does his work."

"I've seen 'm," the secretary said. "He's worked a lot for you."

"All the big little fellows has tried out on him," Roberts answered. "And he's learned from 'em. I've seen some of them he could lick. But his heart wasn't in it. I reckoned he never liked the game. He seemed to act that way."

"He's been fighting some before the little clubs the last few months," Kelly said.

"Sure. But I don't know what struck 'm. All of a sudden his heart got into it. He just went out like a streak and cleaned up all the little local fellows. Seemed to want the money, and he's won a bit, though his clothes don't look it. He's peculiar. Nobody knows his business. Nobody knows how he spends his time. Even when he's on the job, he plumb up and disappears most of each day soon as his work is done. Sometimes he just blows away for weeks at a time. But he don't take advice. There's a fortune in it for the fellow that gets the job of managin' him, only he won't consider it. And you watch him hold out for the cash money when you get down to terms."

It was at this stage that Danny Ward arrived. Quite a party it was. His manager and trainer were with him, and he breezed in like a gusty draught of geniality, good-nature, and all-conqueringness. Greetings flew about, a joke here, a retort there, a smile or a laugh for everybody. Yet it was his way, and only partly sincere. He was a good actor, and he had found geniality a most valuable asset in the game of getting on in the world. But down underneath he was the deliberate, cold-blooded fighter and business man. The rest was a mask. Those who knew him or trafficked with him said that when it came to brass tacks he was Danny-on-the-Spot. He was invariably present at all business discussions, and it was urged by some that his manager was a blind whose only function was to serve as Danny's mouth-piece.

Rivera's way was different. Indian blood, as well as Spanish, was in his veins, and he sat back in a corner, silent, immobile, only his black eyes passing from face to face and noting everything.

"So that's the guy," Danny said, running an appraising eye over his proposed antagonist. "How de do, old chap."

Rivera's eyes burned venomously, but he made no sign of acknowledgment. He disliked all Gringos, but this Gringo he hated with an immediacy that was unusual even in him.

"Gawd!" Danny protested facetiously to the promoter. "You ain't expectin' me to fight a deef mute." When the laughter subsided, he made another hit. "Los Angeles must be on the dink when this is the best you can scare up. What kindergarten did you get 'm from?"

"He's a good little boy, Danny, take it from me," Roberts defended. "Not as easy as he looks."

"And half the house is sold already," Kelly pleaded. "You'll have to take 'm on, Danny. It is the best we can do."

Danny ran another careless and unflattering glance over Rivera and sighed.

"I gotta be easy with 'm, I guess. If only he don't blow up."

Roberts snorted.

"You gotta be careful," Danny's manager warned. "No taking chances with a dub that's likely to sneak a lucky one across."

"Oh, I'll be careful all right, all right," Danny smiled. "I'll get in at the start an' nurse 'im along for the dear public's sake. What d' ye say to fifteen rounds, Kelly—an' then the hay for him?"

"That'll do," was the answer. "As long as you make it realistic."

"Then let's get down to biz." Danny paused and calculated. "Of course, sixty-five per cent of the gate receipts, same as with Carthey. But the split'll be different. Eighty will just about suit me." And to his manager, "That right?"

The manager nodded.

"Here, you, did you get that?" Kelly asked Rivera.

Rivera shook his head.

"Well, it is this way," Kelly exposited. "The purse'll be sixty-five per cent of the gate receipts. You're a dub, and an unknown. You and Danny split, twenty per cent goin' to you, an' eighty to Danny. That's fair, isn't it, Roberts?"

"Very fair, Rivera," Roberts agreed.

"You see, you ain't got a reputation yet."

"What will sixty-five per cent of the gate receipts be?" Rivera demanded.

"Oh, maybe five thousand, maybe as high as eight thousand," Danny broke in to explain. "Something like that. Your share'll come to something like a thousand or sixteen hundred. Pretty good for takin' a licking from a guy with my reputation. What d' ye say?"

Then Rivera took their breaths away. "Winner takes all," he said with finality.

A dead silence prevailed.

"It's like candy from a baby," Danny's manager proclaimed.

Danny shook his head.

"I've been in the game too long," he explained.

"I'm not casting reflections on the referee, or the present company. I'm not sayin' nothing about book-makers an' frame-ups that sometimes happen. But what I do say is that it's poor business for a fighter like me. I play safe. There's no tellin'. Mebbe I break my arm, eh? Or some guy slips me a bunch of dope?" He shook his head solemnly. "Win or lose, eighty is my split. What d' ye say, Mexican?"

Rivera shook his head.

Danny exploded. He was getting down to brass tacks now.

"Why, you dirty little greaser! I've a mind to knock your block off right now."

Roberts drawled his body to interposition between hostilities.

"Winner takes all," Rivera repeated sullenly.

"Why do you stand out that way?" Danny asked.

"I can lick you," was the straight answer.

Danny half started to take off his coat. But, as his manager knew, it was a grand stand play. The coat did not come off, and Danny allowed himself to be placated by the group. Everybody sympathized with him. Rivera stood alone.

"Look here, you little fool," Kelly took up the argument. "You're nobody. We know what you've been doing the last few months—putting away little local fighters. But Danny is class. His next fight after this will be for the championship. And you're unknown. Nobody ever heard of you out of Los Angeles."

"They will," Rivera answered with a shrug, "after this fight."

"You think for a second you can lick me?" Danny blurted in.

Rivera nodded.

"Oh, come; listen to reason," Kelly pleaded. "Think of the advertising."

"I want the money," was Rivera's answer.

"You couldn't win from me in a thousand years," Danny assured him.

"Then what are you holdin' out for?" Rivera

countered. "If the money's that easy, why don't you go after it?"

"I will, so help me!" Danny cried with abrupt conviction. "I'll beat you to death in the ring, my boy—you monkeyin' with me this way. Make out the articles, Kelly. Winner take all. Play it up in the sportin' columns. Tell 'em it's a grudge fight. I'll show this fresh kid a few."

Kelly's secretary had begun to write, when Danny interrupted.

"Hold on!" He turned to Rivera.

"Weights?"

"Ringside," came the answer.

"Not on your life, Fresh Kid. If winner takes all, we weigh in at ten A.M."

"And winner takes all?" Rivera queried.

Danny nodded. That settled it. He would enter the ring in his full ripeness of strength.

"Weigh in at ten," Rivera said.

The secretary's pen went on scratching.

"It means five pounds," Roberts complained to Rivera.

"You've given too much away. You've thrown the fight right there. Danny'll lick you sure. He'll be as strong as a bull. You're a fool. You ain't got the chance of a dewdrop in hell."

Rivera's answer was a calculated look of hatred. Even this Gringo he despised, and him had he found the whitest Gringo of them all.

CHAPTER 4

BARLEY NOTICED was Rivera as he entered the ring. Only a very slight and very scattering ripple of half-hearted hand-clapping greeted him. The house did not believe in him. He was the lamb led to slaughter at the hands of the great Danny. Besides, the house was disappointed. It had expected a rushing battle between Danny Ward and Billy Carthey, and here it must put up with this poor little tyro. Still further, it had manifested its disapproval of the change by betting two, and even three, to one on Danny. And where a betting audience's money is, there is its heart.

The Mexican boy sat down in his corner and waited. The slow minutes lagged by. Danny was making him wait. It was an old trick, but ever it worked on the young, new fighters. They grew frightened, sitting thus and facing their own apprehensions and a callous, tobacco-smoking audience. But for once the trick failed. Roberts was right. Rivera had no goat. He, who was more delicately coordinated, more finely nerved and strung than any of them, had no nerves of this sort. The atmosphere of foredoomed defeat in his own corner had no effect on him. His handlers were Gringos and strangers. Also they were scrubs—the dirty driftage of the fight game, without honor, without efficiency. And they were chilled, as well, with certitude that theirs was the losing corner.

"Now you gotta be careful," Spider Hagerty warned him. Spider was his chief second. "Make it last as long as you can—them's my instructions from Kelly. If you don't, the papers'll call it another bum fight and give the game a bigger black eye in Los Angeles."

All of which was not encouraging. But Rivera took no notice. He despised prize fighting. It was the hated game of the hated Gringo. He had taken up with it, as a chopping block for others in the training quarters, solely because he was starving. The fact that he was marvelously made for it had meant nothing. He hated it. Not until he had come in to the Junta, had he fought for money, and he had found the money easy. Not first among the sons of men had he been to find himself successful at a despised vocation.

He did not analyze. He merely knew that he must win this fight. There could be no other outcome. For behind him, nerving him to this belief, were profounder forces than any the crowded house dreamed. Danny Ward fought for money, and for the easy ways of life that money would bring. But the things Rivera fought for burned in his brain—blazing and terrible visions, that, with eyes wide open, sitting lonely in the corner of the ring and waiting for his tricky antagonist, he saw as clearly as he had lived them.

He saw the white-walled, water-power factories of Rio Blanco. He saw the six thousand workers, starved and wan, and the little children, seven and eight years of age, who toiled long shifts for ten cents a day. He saw the perambulating corpses, the ghastly death's heads of men who labored in the dye-rooms. He remembered that he had heard his father call the dye-rooms the "suicide-holes," where a year was death. He saw the little patio, and his mother cooking and moiling at crude housekeeping and finding time to caress and love him. And his father he saw, large, big-moustached and deep-chested, kindly above all men, who loved all men and whose heart was so large that there was love to overflowing still left for the mother and the little muchacho playing in the corner of the patio. In those days his name had not been Felipe Rivera. It had been Fernandez, his father's and mother's name. Him had they called Juan. Later, he had changed it himself, for he had found the name of Fernandez hated by prefects of police, jefes politicos, and rurales.

Big, hearty Joaquin Fernandez! A large place he occupied in Rivera's visions. He had not understood at the time, but looking back he could understand. He could see him setting type in the little printery, or scribbling endless hasty, nervous lines on the much-cluttered desk. And he could see the strange evenings, when workmen, coming secretly in the dark like men who did ill deeds, met with his father and talked long hours where he, the muchacho, lay not always asleep in the corner.

As from a remote distance he could hear Spider Hagerty saying to him: "No layin' down at the start. Them's instructions. Take a beatin' and earn your dough."

Ten minutes had passed, and he still sat in his

corner. There were no signs of Danny, who was evidently playing the trick to the limit.

But more visions burned before the eye of Rivera's memory. The strike, or, rather, the lockout, because the workers of Rio Blanco had helped their striking brothers of Puebla. The hunger, the expeditions in the hills for berries, the roots and herbs that all ate and that twisted and pained the stomachs of all of them. And then, the nightmare; the waste of ground before the company's store; the thousands of starving workers; General Rosalio Martinez and the soldiers of Porfirio Diaz, and the death-spitting rifles that seemed never to cease spitting, while the workers' wrongs were washed and washed again in their own blood. And that night! He saw the flat cars, piled high with the bodies of the slain, consigned to Vera Cruz, food for the sharks of the bay. Again he crawled over the grisly heaps, seeking and finding, stripped and mangled, his father and his mother. His mother he especially remembered—only her face projecting, her body burdened by the weight of dozens of bodies. Again the rifles of the soldiers of Porfirio Diaz cracked, and again he dropped to the ground and slunk away like some hunted coyote of the hills.

To his ears came a great roar, as of the sea, and he saw Danny Ward, leading his retinue of trainers and seconds, coming down the center aisle. The house was in wild uproar for the popular hero who was bound to win. Everybody proclaimed him. Everybody was for him. Even Rivera's own seconds warmed to something akin to cheerfulness when Danny ducked jauntily through the ropes and entered the ring. His face continually spread to an unending succession of smiles, and when Danny smiled he smiled in every feature, even to the laughter-wrinkles of the corners of the eyes and into the depths of the eyes themselves. Never was there so genial a fighter. His face was a running advertisement of good feeling, of good fellowship. He knew everybody. He joked, and laughed, and greeted his friends through the ropes. Those farther away, unable to suppress their admiration, cried loudly: "Oh, you Danny!" It was a joyous ovation of affection that lasted a full five minutes.

Rivera was disregarded. For all that the audience noticed, he did not exist. Spider Lagerty's bloated face bent down close to his.

"No gettin' scared," the Spider warned.

"An' remember instructions. You gotta last. No layin' down. If you lay down, we got instructions to beat you up in the dressing rooms. Savve? You just gotta fight."

The house began to applaud. Danny was crossing the ring to him. Danny bent over, caught Rivera's right hand in both his own and shook it with impulsive heartiness. Danny's smile-wreathed face was close to his. The audience yelled its appreciation of Danny's display of sporting spirit. He was greeting his opponent with the fondness of a brother. Danny's lips moved, and the audience, interpreting the unheard words to be those of a kindly-natured sport, yelled again. Only Rivera heard the low words.

"You little Mexican rat," hissed from between Danny's gaily smiling lips, "I'll fetch the yellow outa you."

Rivera made no move. He did not rise. He merely hated with his eyes.

"Get up, you dog!" some man yelled through the ropes from behind.

The crowd began to hiss and boo him for his unsportsmanlike conduct, but he sat unmoved. Another great outburst of applause was Danny's as he walked back across the ring.

When Danny stripped, there was ohs! and ahs! of delight. His body was perfect, alive with easy suppleness and health and strength. The skin was white as a woman's, and as smooth. All grace, and resilience, and power resided therein. He had proved it in scores of battles. His photographs were in all the physical culture magazines.

A groan went up as Spider Hagerty peeled Rivera's sweater over his head. His body seemed leaner, because of the swarthiness of the skin. He had muscles, but they made no display like his opponent's. What the audience neglected to see was the deep chest. Nor could it guess the toughness of the fiber of the flesh, the instantaneousness of the cell explosions of the muscles, the fineness of the nerves that wired every part of him into a splendid fighting mechanism. All the audience saw was a brown-skinned boy of eighteen with what seemed the body of a boy. With Danny it was different. Danny was a man of twenty-four, and his body was a man's body. The contrast was still more striking as they stood together in the center of the ring receiving the referee's last instructions.

Rivera noticed Roberts sitting directly behind the newspaper men. He was drunker than usual, and his speech was correspondingly slower.

"Take it easy, Rivera," Roberts drawled.

"He can't kill you, remember that. He'll rush you at the go-off, but don't get rattled. You just and stall, and clinch. He can't hurt cover up, much. Just make believe to yourself that he's choppin' out on you at the trainin' quarters."

Rivera made no sign that he had heard.

"Sullen little devil," Roberts muttered to the man next to him. "He always was that way."

But Rivera forgot to look his usual hatred. A vision of countless rifles blinded his eyes. Every face in the audience, far as he could see, to the high dollar-seats, was transformed into a rifle. And he saw the long Mexican border arid and sun-washed and aching, and along it he saw the ragged bands that delayed only for the guns.

Back in his corner he waited, standing up. His seconds had crawled out through the ropes, taking the canvas stool with them. Diagonally across the squared ring, Danny faced him. The gong struck, and the battle was on. The audience howled its delight. Never had it seen a battle open more convincingly. The papers were right. It was a grudge fight. Three-quarters of the distance Danny covered in the rush to get together, his intention to eat up the Mexican lad plainly advertised. He assailed with not one blow, nor two, nor a dozen. He was a gyroscope of blows, a whirlwind of destruction. Rivera was nowhere. He was overwhelmed, buried beneath avalanches of punches delivered from every angle and position by a past master in the art. He was overborne, swept back against the ropes, separated by the referee, and swept back against the ropes again.

It was not a fight. It was a slaughter, a massacre. Any audience, save a prize fighting one, would have exhausted its emotions in that first minute. Danny was certainly showing what he could do—a splendid exhibition. Such was the certainty of the audience, as well as its excitement and favoritism, that it failed to take notice that the Mexican still stayed on his feet. It forgot Rivera. It rarely saw him, so closely was he enveloped in Danny's man-eating attack. A minute of this went by, and two minutes. Then, in a separation, it caught a clear glimpse of the Mexican. His lip was cut, his nose was bleeding. As he turned and staggered into a clinch, the welts of oozing blood, from his contacts with the ropes, showed in red bars across his back. But what the audience did not notice was that his chest was not heaving and that his eyes were coldly burning as ever. Too many aspiring champions, in the cruel welter of the training camps, had practiced this man-eating attack on him. He had learned to live through for a compensation of from half a dollar a go up to fifteen dollars a week—a hard school, and he was schooled hard.

Then happened the amazing thing. The whirling, blurring mix-up ceased suddenly. Rivera stood alone. Danny, the redoubtable Danny, lay on his back. His body quivered as consciousness strove to return to it. He had not staggered and sunk down, nor had he gone over in a long slumping fall. The right hook of Rivera had dropped him in midair with the abruptness of death. The referee shoved Rivera back with one hand, and stood over the fallen gladiator counting the seconds. It is the custom of prize-fighting audiences to cheer a clean knock-down blow. But this audience did not cheer. The thing had been too unexpected. It watched the toll of the seconds in tense silence, and through this silence the voice of Roberts rose exultantly:

"I told you he was a two-handed fighter!"

By the fifth second, Danny was rolling over on his face, and when seven was counted, he rested on one knee, ready to rise after the count of nine and before the count of ten. If his knee still touched the floor at "ten," he was considered "down," and also "out." The instant his knee left the floor, he was considered "up," and in that instant it was Rivera's right to try and put him down again. Rivera took no chances. The moment that knee left the floor he would strike again. He circled around, but the referee circled in between, and Rivera knew that the seconds he counted were very slow. All Gringos were against him, even the referee.

At "nine" the referee gave Rivera a sharp thrust back. It was unfair, but it enabled Danny to rise, the smile back on his lips. Doubled partly over, with arms wrapped about face and abdomen, he cleverly stumbled into a clinch. By all the rules of the game the referee should have broken it, but he did not, and Danny clung on like a surf-battered barnacle and moment by moment recuperated. The last minute of the round was going fast. If he could live to the end, he would have a full minute in his corner to revive. And live to the end he did, smiling through all desperateness and extremity.

"The smile that won't come off!" somebody yelled, and the audience laughed loudly in its relief.

"The kick that Greaser's got is something God-awful," Danny gasped in his corner to his adviser while his handlers worked frantically over him.

The second and third rounds were tame. Danny, a tricky and consummate ring general, stalled and blocked and held on, devoting himself to recovering from that dazing first-round blow. In the fourth round he was himself again. Jarred and shaken, nevertheless his good condition had enabled him to regain his vigor. But he tried no man-eating tactics. The Mexican had proved a tartar. Instead, he brought to bear his best fighting powers. In tricks and skill and experience he was the master, and though he could land nothing vital, he proceeded scientifically to chop and wear down his opponent. He landed three blows to Rivera's one, but they were punishing blows only, and not deadly. It was the sum of many of them that constituted deadliness. He was respectful of this two-handed dub with the amazing short-arm kicks in both his fists.

In defense, Rivera developed a disconcerting straight-left. Again and again, attack after attack he straight-lefted away from him with accumulated damage to Danny's mouth and nose. But Danny was protean. That was why he was the coming champion. He could change from style to style of fighting at will. He now devoted himself to infighting. In this he was particularly wicked, and it enabled him to avoid the other's straight-left. Here he set the house wild repeatedly, capping it with a marvelous lockbreak and lift of an inside upper-cut that raised the Mexican in the air and dropped him to the mat. Rivera rested on one knee, making the most of the count, and in the soul of him he knew the referee was counting short seconds on him.

Again, in the seventh, Danny achieved the diabolical

inside uppercut. He succeeded only in staggering Rivera, but, in the ensuing moment of defenseless helplessness, he smashed him with another blow through the ropes. Rivera's body bounced on the heads of the newspaper men below, and they boosted him back to the edge of the platform outside the ropes. Here he rested on one knee, while the referee raced off the seconds. Inside the ropes, through which he must duck to enter the ring, Danny waited for him. Nor did the referee intervene or thrust Danny back.

The house was beside itself with delight.

"Kill'm, Danny, kill'm!" was the cry.

Scores of voices took it up until it was like a war-chant of wolves.

Danny did his best, but Rivera, at the count of eight, instead of nine, came unexpectedly through the ropes and safely into a clinch. Now the referee worked, tearing him away so that he could be hit, giving Danny every advantage that an unfair referee can give.

But Rivera lived, and the daze cleared from his brain. It was all of a piece. They were the hated Gringos and they were all unfair. And in the worst of it visions continued to flash and sparkle in his brain—long lines of railroad track that simmered across the desert; rurales and American constables, prisons and calabooses; tramps at water tanks—all the squalid and painful panorama of his odyssey after Rio Blanca and the strike. And, resplendent and glorious, he saw the great, red Revolution sweeping across his land. The guns were there before him. Every hated face was a gun. It was for the guns he fought. He was the guns. He was the Revolution. He fought for all Mexico.

The audience began to grow incensed with Rivera. Why didn't he take the licking that was appointed him? Of course he was going to be licked, but why should he be so obstinate about it? Very few were interested in him, and they were the certain, definite percentage of a gambling crowd that plays long shots. Believing Danny to be the winner, nevertheless they had put their money on the Mexican at four to ten and one to three. More than a trifle was up on the point of how many rounds Rivera could last. Wild money had appeared at the ringside proclaiming that he could not last seven rounds, or even six. The winners of this, now that their cash risk was happily settled, had joined in cheering on the favorite.

Rivera refused to be licked. Through the eighth round his opponent strove vainly to repeat the uppercut. In the ninth, Rivera stunned the house again. In the midst of a clinch he broke the lock with a quick, lithe movement, and in the narrow space between their bodies his right lifted from the waist. Danny went to the floor and took the safety of the count. The crowd was appalled. He was being bested at his own game. His famous right-uppercut had been worked back on him. Rivera made no attempt to catch him as he arose at "nine." The referee was openly blocking that play, though he stood clear when the situation was reversed and it was Rivera who desired to rise.

Twice in the tenth, Rivera put through the right-uppercut, lifted from waist to opponent's chin. Danny grew desperate. The smile never left his face, but he went back to his man-eating rushes. Whirlwind as he would, he could not damage Rivera, while Rivera through the blur and whirl, dropped him to the mat three times in succession. Danny did not recuperate so quickly now, and by the eleventh round he was in a serious way. But from then till the fourteenth he put up the gamest exhibition of his career. He stalled and blocked, fought parsimoniously, and strove to gather strength. Also, he fought as foully as a successful fighter knows how. Every trick and device he employed, butting in the clinches with the seeming of accident, pinioning Rivera's glove between arm and body, heeling his glove on Rivera's mouth to clog his breathing. Often, in the clinches, through his cut and smiling lips he snarled insults unspeakable and vile in Rivera's ear. Everybody, from the referee to the house, was with Danny and was helping Danny. And they knew what he had in mind. Bested by this surprise-box of an unknown, he was pinning all on a single punch. He offered himself for punishment, fished, and feinted, and drew, for that one opening that would enable him to whip a blow through with all his strength and turn the tide. As another and greater fighter had done before him, he might do a right and left, to solar plexus and across the jaw. He could do it, for he was noted for the strength of punch that remained in his arms as long as he could keep his feet.

Rivera's seconds were not half-caring for him in the intervals between rounds. Their towels made a showing, but drove little air into his panting lungs. Spider Hagerty talked advice to him, but Rivera knew it was wrong advice. Everybody was against him. He was surrounded by treachery. In the fourteenth round he put Danny down again, and himself stood resting, hands dropped at side, while the referee counted. In the other corner Rivera had been noting suspicious whisperings. He saw Michael Kelly make his way to Roberts and bend and whisper. Rivera's ears were a cat's, desert-trained, and he caught snatches of what was said. He wanted to hear more, and when his opponent arose he maneuvered the fight into a clinch over against the ropes.

"Got to," he could hear Michael, while Roberts nodded. "Danny's got to win—I stand to lose a mint—I've got a ton of money covered—my own. If he lasts the fifteenth I'm bust—the boy'll mind you. Put something across."

And thereafter Rivera saw no more visions. They were trying to job him. Once again he dropped Danny and stood resting, his hands at his slide. Roberts stood up.

"That settled him," he said.

"Go to your corner."

He spoke with authority, as he had often spoken to Rivera at the training quarters. But Rivera looked hatred at him and waited for Danny to rise. Back in his corner in the minute interval, Kelly, the promoter, came and talked to Rivera.

"Throw it, damn you," he rasped in, a harsh low voice. "You gotta lay down, Rivera. Stick with me and I'll make your future. I'll let you lick Danny next time. But here's where you lay down."

Rivera showed with his eyes that he heard, but he made neither sign of assent nor dissent.

"Why don't you speak?" Kelly demanded angrily.

"You lose, anyway," Spider Hagerty supplemented. "The referee'll take it away from you. Listen to Kelly, and lay down."

"Lay down, kid," Kelly pleaded, "and I'll help you to the championship."

Rivera did not answer.

"I will, so help me, kid."

At the strike of the gong Rivera sensed something impending. The house did not. Whatever it was it was there inside the ring with him and very close. Danny's earlier surety seemed returned to him. The confidence of his advance frightened Rivera. Some trick was about to be worked. Danny rushed, but Rivera refused the encounter. He side-stepped away into safety. What the other wanted was a clinch. It was in some way necessary to the trick. Rivera backed and circled away, yet he knew, sooner or later, the clinch and the trick would come. Desperately he resolved to draw it. He made as if to effect the clinch with Danny's next rush. Instead, at the last instant, just as their bodies should have come together, Rivera darted nimbly back. And in the same instant Danny's corner raised a cry of foul. Rivera had fooled them. The referee paused irresolutely. The decision that trembled on his lips was never uttered, for a shrill, boy's voice from the gallery piped, "Raw work!"

Danny cursed Rivera openly, and forced him, while Rivera danced away. Also, Rivera made up his mind to strike no more blows at the body. In this he threw away half his chance of winning, but he knew if he was to win at all it was with the outfighting that remained to him. Given the least opportunity, they would lie a foul on him. Danny threw all caution to the winds. For two rounds he tore after and into the boy who dared not meet him at close quarters. Rivera was struck again and again; he took blows by the dozens to avoid the perilous clinch. During this supreme final rally of Danny's the audience rose to its feet and went mad. It did not understand. All it could see was that its favorite was winning, after all.

"Why don't you fight?" it demanded wrathfully of Rivera.

"You're yellow! You're yellow!" "Open up, you cur! Open up!" "Kill'm, Danny! Kill 'm!" "You sure got 'm! Kill 'm!"

In all the house, bar none, Rivera was the only cold man. By temperament and blood he was the hottest-passioned there; but he had gone through such vastly greater heats that this collective passion of ten thousand throats, rising surge on surge, was to his brain no more than the velvet cool of a summer twilight.

Into the seventeenth round Danny carried his rally. Rivera, under a heavy blow, drooped and sagged. His hands dropped helplessly as he reeled backward. Danny thought it was his chance. The boy was at, his mercy. Thus Rivera, feigning, caught him off his guard, lashing out a clean drive to the mouth. Danny went down. When he arose, Rivera felled him with a down-chop of the right on neck and jaw. Three times he repeated this. It was impossible for any referee to call these blows foul.

"Oh, Bill! Bill!" Kelly pleaded to the referee.

"I can't," that official lamented back. "He won't give me a chance."

Danny, battered and heroic, still kept coming up. Kelly and others near to the ring began to cry out to the police to stop it, though Danny's corner refused to throw in the towel. Rivera saw the fat police captain starting awkwardly to climb through the ropes, and was not sure what it meant. There were so many ways of cheating in this game of the Gringos. Danny, on his feet, tottered groggily and helplessly before him. The referee and the captain were both reaching for Rivera when he struck the last blow. There was no need to stop the fight, for Danny did not rise.

"Count!" Rivera cried hoarsely to the referee.

And when the count was finished, Danny's seconds gathered him up and carried him to his corner.

"Who wins?" Rivera demanded.

Reluctantly, the referee caught his gloved hand and held it aloft.

There were no congratulations for Rivera. He walked to his corner unattended, where his seconds had not yet placed his stool. He leaned backward on the ropes and looked his hatred at them, swept it on and about him till the whole ten thousand Gringos were included. His knees trembled under him, and he was sobbing from exhaustion. Before his eyes the hated faces swayed back and forth in the giddiness of nausea. Then he remembered they were the guns. The guns were his. The Revolution could go on.

THE ABYSMAL BRUTE

CHAPTER 1

SAM STUBENER RAN THROUGH HIS MAIL carelessly and rapidly. As became a manager of prize-fighters, he was accustomed to a various and bizarre correspondence. Every crank, sport, near sport, and reformer seemed to have ideas to impart to him. From dire threats against his life to milder threats, such as pushing in the front of his face, from rabbit-foot fetishes to lucky horse-shoes, from dinky jerkwater bids to the quarter-of-a-million-dollar offers of irresponsible nobodies, he knew the whole run of the surprise portion of his mail. In his time having received a razor-strop made from the skin of a lynched negro, and a finger, withered and sun-dried, cut from the body of a white man found in Death Valley, he was of the opinion that never again would the postman bring him anything that could startle him. But this morning he opened a letter that he read a second time, put away in his pocket, and took out for a third reading. It was postmarked from some unheard-of post-office in Siskiyou County, and it ran:

Dear Sam:

> *You don't know me, except my reputation. You come after my time, and I've been out of the game a long time. But take it from me I ain't been asleep. I've followed the whole game, and I've followed you, from the time Kal Aufman knocked you out to your last handling of Nat Belson, and I take it you're the niftiest thing in the line of managers that ever came down the pike.*
>
> *I got a proposition for you. I got the greatest unknown that ever happened. This ain't con. It's the straight goods. What do you think of a husky that tips the scales at two hundred and twenty pounds fighting weight, is twenty-two years old, and can hit a kick twice as hard as my best ever? That's him, my boy, Young Pat Glendon, that's the name he'll fight under. I've planned it all out. Now the best thing you can do is hit the first train and come up here.*
>
> *I bred him and I trained him. All that I ever had in my head I've hammered into his. And maybe you won't believe it, but he's added to it. He's a born fighter. He's a wonder at time and distance. He just knows to the second and the inch, and he don't have to think about it at all. His six-inch jolt is more the real sleep medicine than the full-arm swing of most geezers.*
>
> *Talk about the hope of the white race. This*

is him. Come and take a peep. When you was managing Jeffries you was crazy about hunting. Come along and I'll give you some real hunting and fishing that will make your moving picture winnings look like thirty cents. I'll send Young Pat out with you. I ain't able to get around. That's why I'm sending for you. I was going to manage him myself. But it ain't no use. I'm all in and likely to pass out any time. So get a move on. I want you to manage him. There's a fortune in it for both of you, but I want to draw up the contract.

Yours truly,
PAT GLENDON.

Stubener was puzzled. It seemed, on the face of it, a joke—the men in the fighting game were notorious jokers—and he tried to discern the fine hand of Corbett or the big friendly paw of Fitzsimmons in the screed before him. But if it were genuine, he knew it was worth looking into. Pat Glendon was before his time, though, as a cub, he had once seen Old Pat spar at the benefit for Jack Dempsey. Even then he was called "Old" Pat, and had been out of the ring for years. He had antedated Sullivan, in the old London Prize Ring Rules, though his last fading battles had been put up under the incoming Marquis of Queensbury Rules.

What ring-follower did not know of Pat Glendon?—though few were alive who had seen him in his prime, and there were not many more who had seen him at all. Yet his name had come down in the history of the ring, and no sporting writer's lexicon was complete without it.

His fame was paradoxical. No man was honored higher, and yet he had never attained championship honors. He had been unfortunate, and had been known as the unlucky fighter.

Four times he all but won the heavyweight championship, and each time he had deserved to win it. There was the time on the barge, in San Francisco Bay, when, at the moment he had the champion going, he snapped his own forearm; and on the island in the Thames, sloshing about in six inches of rising tide, he broke a leg at a similar stage in a winning fight; in Texas, too, there was the never-to-be-forgotten day when the police broke in just as he had his man going in all certainty. And finally, there was the fight in the Mechanics' Pavilion in San Francisco, when he was secretly jobbed from the first by a gun-fighting bad man of a referee backed by a small syndicate of bettors. Pat Glendon had had no accidents in that fight, but when he had knocked his man cold with a right to the jaw and a left to the solar plexus, the referee calmly disqualified him for fouling. Every ringside witness, every sporting expert, and the whole sporting world, knew there had been no foul. Yet, like all fighters, Pat Glendon had agreed to abide by the decision of the referee. Pat abided, and accepted it as in keeping with the rest of his bad luck.

This was Pat Glendon. What bothered Stubener was whether or not Pat had written the letter. He carried it down town with him. What's become of Pat Glendon? Such was his greeting to all sports that morning. Nobody seemed to know. Some thought he must be dead, but none knew positively. The fight editor of a morning daily looked up the records and was able to state that his death had not been noted. It was from Tim Donovan, that he got a clue.

"Sure an' he ain't dead," said Donovan. "How could that be?—a man of his make that never boozed or blew himself? He made money, and what's more, he saved it and invested it. Didn't he have three saloons at the one time? An' wasn't he makin' slathers of money with them when he sold out? Now that I'm thinkin', that was the last time I laid eyes on him—when he sold them out. 'Twas all of twenty years and more ago. His wife had just died. I met him headin' for the Ferry. 'Where away, old sport?' says I. 'It's me for the woods,' says he. 'I've   quit. Good-by, Tim, me boy.' And I've never seen him from that day to this. Of course he ain't dead."

"You say when his wife died—did he have any children?" Stubener queried.

"One, a little baby. He was luggin' it in his arms that very day."

"Was it a boy?"

"How should I be knowin'?"

It was then that Sam Stubener reached a decision, and that night found him in a Pullman speeding toward the wilds of Northern California.

CHAPTER 2

STUBENER WAS DROPPED OFF the overland at Deer Lick in the early morning, and he kicked his heels for an hour before the one saloon opened its doors. No, the saloonkeeper didn't know anything about Pat Glendon, had never heard of him, and if he was in that part of the country he must be out beyond somewhere. Neither had the one hanger-on ever heard of Pat Glendon. At the hotel the same ignorance obtained, and it was not until the storekeeper and postmaster opened up that Stubener struck the trail. Oh, yes, Pat Glendon lived out beyond. You took the stage at Alpine, which was forty miles and which was a logging camp. From Alpine, on horseback, you rode up Antelope Valley and crossed the divide to Bear Creek. Pat Glendon lived somewhere beyond that. The people of Alpine would know. Yes, there was a young Pat. The storekeeper had seen him. He had been in to Deer Lick two years back. Old Pat had not put in an appearance for five years. He bought his supplies at the store, and always paid by check, and he was a white-haired, strange old man. That was all the storekeeper knew, but the folks at Alpine could give him final directions.

It looked good to Stubener. Beyond doubt there was a young Pat Glendon, as well as an old one, living out beyond. That night the manager spent at the logging camp of Alpine, and early the following morning he rode a mountain cayuse up Antelope Valley. He rode over the divide and down Bear Creek. He rode all day, through the wildest, roughest country he had ever seen, and at sunset turned up Pinto Valley on a trail so stiff and narrow that more than once he elected to get off and walk.

It was eleven o'clock when he dismounted before a log cabin and was greeted by the baying of two huge deer-hounds. Then Pat Glendon opened the door, fell on his neck, and took him in.

"I knew ye'd come, Sam, me boy," said Pat, the while he limped about, building a fire, boiling coffee, and frying a big bear-steak. "The young un ain't home the night. We was gettin' short of meat, and he went out about sundown to pick up a deer. But I'll say no more. Wait till ye see him. He'll be home in the morn, and then you can try him out. There's the gloves. But wait till ye see him.

"As for me, I'm finished. Eighty-one come next January, an' pretty good for an ex-bruiser. But I never wasted meself, Sam, nor kept late hours an' burned the candle at all ends. I had a damned good candle, an' made the most of it, as you'll grant at lookin' at me. And I've taught the same to the young un. What do you think of a lad of twenty-two that's never had a drink in his life nor tasted tobacco? That's him. He's a giant, and he's lived natural all his days. Wait till he takes you out after deer. He'll break your heart travelin' light, him a carryin' the outfit and a big buck deer belike. He's a child of the open air, an' winter nor summer has he slept under a roof. The open for him, as I taught him. The one thing that worries me is how he'll take to sleepin' in houses, an' how he'll stand the tobacco smoke in the ring. 'Tis a terrible thing, that smoke, when you're fighting hard an' gaspin' for air. But no more, Sam, me boy. You're tired an' sure should be sleepin'. Wait till you see him, that's all. Wait till you see him."

But the garrulousness of age was on old Pat, and it was long before he permitted Stubener's eyes to close.

"He can run a deer down with his own legs, that young un," he broke out again. "'Tis the dandy trainin' for the lungs, the hunter's life. He don't know much of else, though, he's read a few books at times an' poetry stuff. He's just plain pure natural, as you'll see when you clap eyes on him. He's got the old Irish strong in him. Sometimes, the way he moons about, it's thinkin' strong I am that he believes in the fairies and such-like. He's a nature lover if ever there was one, an' he's afeard of cities. He's read about them, but the biggest he was ever in was Deer Lick. He misliked the many people, and his report was that they'd stand weedin' out. That was two years agone—the first and the last time he's seen a locomotive and a train of cars.

"Sometimes it's wrong I'm thinkin' I am, bringin' him up a natural. It's given him wind and stamina and the strength o' wild bulls. No city-grown man can have a look-in against him. I'm willin' to grant that Jeffries at his best could 'a' worried the young un a bit, but only a bit. The young un could 'a' broke him like a straw. An' he don't look it. That's the everlasting wonder of it. He's only a fine-seeming young husky; but it's the quality of his muscle that's different. But wait till ye see him, that's all.

"A strange liking the boy has for posies, an' little meadows, a bit of pine with the moon beyond, windy sunsets, or the sun o' morns from the top of old Baldy. An' he has a hankerin' for the drawin' o' pitchers of things, an' of spouting about 'Lucifer or night' from the poetry books he got from the red-headed school teacher. But 'tis only his youngness. He'll settle down to the game once we get him started, but watch out for grouches when it first comes to livin' in a city for him.

"A good thing; he's woman-shy. They'll not bother him for years. He can't bring himself to understand the creatures, an' damn few of them has he seen at that. 'Twas the school teacher over at Samson's Flat that put the poetry stuff in his head. She was clean daffy over the young un, an' he never a-knowin'. A warm-haired girl she was—not a mountain girl, but from down in the flat-lands—an' as time went by she was fair desperate, an' the way she went after him was shameless. An' what d'ye think the boy did when he tumbled to it? He was scared as a jackrabbit. He took blankets an' ammunition an' hiked for tall timber. Not for a month did I lay eyes on him, an' then he sneaked in after dark and was gone in the morn. Nor would he as much as peep at her letters. 'Burn 'em,' he said. An' burn 'em I did. Twice she rode over on a cayuse all the way from Samson's Flat, an' I was sorry for the young creature. She was fair hungry for the boy, and she looked it in her face. An' at the end of three months she gave up school an' went back to her own country, an' then it was that the boy came home to the shack to live again.

"Women ha' ben the ruination of many a good fighter, but they won't be of him. He blushes like a girl if anything young in skirts looks at him a second time or too long the first one. An' they all look at him. But when he fights, when he fights!—God! it's the old savage Irish that flares in him, an' drives the fists of him. Not that he goes off his base. Don't walk away with that. At my best I was never as cool as he. I misdoubt 'twas the wrath of me that brought the accidents. But he's an iceberg. He's hot an' cold at the one time, a live wire in an ice-chest."

Stubener was dozing, when the old man's mumble aroused him. He listened drowsily.

"I made a man o' him, by God! I made a man o' him, with the two fists of him, an' the upstanding legs of him, an' the straight-seein' eyes. And I know the game in my head, an' I've kept up with the times and the modern changes. The crouch? Sure, he knows all the styles an' economies. He never moves two inches when an inch and a half will do the turn. And when he wants he can spring like a buck kangaroo. In-fightin'? Wait till you see. Better than his out-fightin', and he could sure 'a' sparred with Peter Jackson an' outfooted Corbett in his best. I tell you, I've taught'm it all, to the last trick, and he's improved on the teachin'. He's a fair genius at the game. An' he's had plenty of husky mountain men to try out on. I gave him the fancy work and they gave him the sloggin'. Nothing shy or delicate about them. Roarin' bulls an' big grizzly bears, that's what they are, when it comes to huggin' in a clinch or swingin' rough-like in the rushes. An' he plays with 'em. Man, d'ye hear me?—he plays with them, like you an' me would play with little puppy-dogs."

Another time Stubener awoke, to hear the old man mumbling:

"'Tis the funny think he don't take fightin' seriously. It's that easy to him he thinks it play. But wait till he's tapped a swift one. That's all, wait. An' you'll see'm throw on the juice in that cold storage plant of his an' turn loose the prettiest scientific wallopin' that ever you laid eyes on."

In the shivery gray of mountain dawn, Stubener was routed from his blankets by old Pat.

"He's comin' up the trail now," was the hoarse whisper. "Out with ye an' take your first peep at the biggest fightin' man the ring has ever seen, or will ever see in a thousand years again."

The manager peered through the open door, rubbing the sleep from his heavy eyes, and saw a young giant walk into the clearing. In one hand was a rifle, across his shoulders a heavy deer under which he moved as if it were weightless. He was dressed roughly in blue overalls and woolen shirt open at the throat. Coat he had none, and on his feet, instead of brogans, were moccasins. Stubener noted that his walk was smooth and catlike, without suggestion of his two hundred and twenty pounds of weight to which that of the deer was added. The fight manager was impressed from the first glimpse. Formidable the young fellow certainly was, but the manager sensed the strangeness and unusualness of him. He was a new type, something different from the run of fighters. He seemed a creature of the wild, more a night-roaming figure from some old fairy story or folk tale than a twentieth-century youth.

A thing Stubener quickly discovered was that young Pat was not much of a talker. He acknowledged old Pat's introduction with a grip of the hand but without speech, and silently set to work at building the fire and getting breakfast. To his father's direct questions he answered in monosyllables, as, for instance, when asked where he had picked up the deer.

"South Fork," was all he vouchsafed.

"Eleven miles across the mountains," the old man exposited pridefully to Stubener, "an' a trail that'd break your heart."

Breakfast consisted of black coffee, sourdough bread, and an immense quantity of bear-meat broiled over the coals. Of this the young fellow ate ravenously, and Stubener divined that both the Glendons were accustomed to an almost straight meat diet. Old Pat did all the talking, though it was not till the meal was ended that he broached the subject he had at heart.

"Pat, boy," he began, "you know who the gentleman is?"

Young Pat nodded, and cast a quick, comprehensive glance at the manager.

"Well, he'll be takin' you away with him and down to San Francisco."

"I'd sooner stay here, dad," was the answer.

Stubener felt a prick of disappointment. It was a wild goose chase after all. This was no fighter, eager and fretting to be at it. His huge brawn counted for nothing. It was nothing new. It was the big fellows that usually had the streak of fat.

But old Pat's Celtic wrath flared up, and his voice was harsh with command.

"You'll go down to the cities an' fight, me boy. That's what I've trained you for, an' you'll do it."

"All right," was the unexpected response, rumbled apathetically from the deep chest.

"And fight like hell," the old man added.

Again Stubener felt disappointment at the absence of flash and fire in the young man's eyes as he answered:

"All right. When do we start?"

"Oh, Sam, here, he'll be wantin' a little huntin' and to fish a bit, as well as to try you out with the gloves." He looked at Sam, who nodded. "Suppose you strip and give'm a taste of your quality."

An hour later, Sam Stubener had his eyes opened. An ex-fighter himself, a heavyweight at that, he was even a better judge of fighters, and never had he seen one strip to like advantage.

"See the softness of him," old Pat chanted. "'Tis the true stuff. Look at the slope of the shoulders, an' the lungs of him. Clean, all clean, to the last drop an' ounce of him. You're lookin' at a man, Sam, the like of which was never seen before. Not a muscle of him bound. No weight-lifter or Sandow exercise artist there. See the fat snakes of muscles a-crawlin' soft an' lazy-like. Wait till you see them flashin' like a strikin' rattler. He's good for forty rounds this blessed instant, or a hundred. Go to it! Time!"

They went to it, for three-minute rounds with a

minute rests, and Sam Stubener was immediately undeceived. Here was no streak of fat, no apathy, only a lazy, good-natured play of gloves and tricks, with a brusk stiffness and harsh sharpness in the contacts that he knew belonged only to the trained and instinctive fighting man.

"Easy, now, easy," old Pat warned. "Sam's not the man he used to be."

This nettled Sam, as it was intended to do, and he played his most famous trick and favorite punch—a feint for a clinch and a right rip to the stomach. But, quickly as it was delivered, young Pat saw it, and, though it landed, his body was going away. The next time, his body did not go away. As the rip started, he moved forward and twisted his left hip to meet it. It was only a matter of several inches, yet it blocked the blow. And thereafter, try as he would, Stubener's glove got no farther than that hip.

Stubener had roughed it with big men in his time, and, in exhibition bouts, had creditably held his own. But there was no holding his own here. Young Pat played with him, and in the clinches made him feel as powerful as a baby, landing on him seemingly at will, locking and blocking with masterful accuracy, and scarcely noticing or acknowledging his existence. Half the time young Pat seemed to spend in gazing off and out at the landscape in a dreamy sort of way. And right here Stubener made another mistake. He took it for a trick of old Pat's training, tried to sneak in a short-arm jolt, found his arm in a lightning lock, and had both his ears cuffed for his pains.

"The instinct for a blow," the old man chortled. "'Tis not put on, I'm tellin' you. He is a wiz. He knows a blow without the lookin', when it starts an' where, the speed, an' space, an' niceness of it. An' 'tis nothing I ever showed him. 'Tis inspiration. He was so born."

Once, in a clinch, the fight manager heeled his glove on young Pat's mouth, and there was just a hint of viciousness in the manner of doing it. A moment later, in the next clinch, Sam received the heel of the other's glove on his own mouth. There was nothing snappy about it, but the pressure, stolidly lazy as it was, put his head back till the joints cracked and for the moment he thought his neck was broken. He slacked his body and dropped his arms in token that the bout was over, felt the instant release, and staggered clear.

"He'll—he'll do," he gasped, looking the admiration he lacked the breath to utter.

Old Pat's eyes were brightly moist with pride and triumph.

"An' what will you be thinkin' to happen when some of the gay an' ugly ones tries to rough it on him?" he asked.

"He'll kill them, sure," was Stubener's verdict.

"No; he's too cool for that. But he'll just hurt them some for their dirtiness."

"Let's draw up the contract," said the manager.

"Wait till you know the whole worth of him!" Old Pat answered. "'Tis strong terms I'll be makin' you come to. Go for a deer-hunt with the boy over the hills an' learn the lungs and the legs of him. Then we'll sign up iron-clad and regular."

Stubener was gone two days on that hunt, and he learned all and more than old Pat had promised, and came back a very weary and very humble man. The young fellow's innocence of the world had been startling to the case-hardened manager, but he had found him nobody's fool. Virgin though his mind was, untouched by all save a narrow mountain experience, nevertheless he had proved possession of a natural keenness and shrewdness far beyond the average. In a way he was a mystery to Sam, who could not understand his terrible equanimity of temper. Nothing ruffled him or worried him, and his patience was of an enduring primitiveness. He never swore, not even the futile and emasculated cuss-words of sissy-boys.

"I'd swear all right if I wanted to," he had explained, when challenged by his companion. "But I guess I've never come to needing it. When I do, I'll swear, I suppose."

Old Pat, resolutely adhering to his decision, said good-by at the cabin.

"It won't be long, Pat, boy, when I'll be readin' about you in the papers. I'd like to go along, but I'm afeard it's me for the mountains till the end."

And then, drawing the manager aside, the old man turned loose on him almost savagely.

"Remember what I've ben tellin' ye over an' over. The boy's clean an' he's honest. He knows nothing of the rottenness of the game. I kept it all away from him, I tell you. He don't know the meanin' of fake. He knows only the bravery, an' romance an' glory of fightin', and I've filled him up with tales of the old ring heroes, though little enough, God knows, it's set him afire. Man, man, I'm tellin' you that I clipped the fight columns from the newspapers to keep it 'way from him—him a-thinkin' I was wantin' them for me scrap book. He don't know a man ever lay down or threw a fight. So don't you get him in anything that ain't straight. Don't turn the boy's stomach. That's why I put in the null and void clause. The first rottenness and the contract's broke of itself. No snide division of stake-money; no secret arrangements with the movin' pitcher men for guaranteed distance. There's slathers o' money for the both of you. But play it square or you lose. Understand?

"And whatever you'll be doin' watch out for the women," was old Pat's parting admonishment, young Pat astride his horse and reining in dutifully to hear. "Women is death an' damnation, remember that. But when you do find the one, the only one, hang on to her. She'll be worth more than glory an' money. But first be sure, an' when you're sure, don't let her slip through your fingers. Grab her with the two hands of you and hang on. Hang on if all the world goes to smash an' smithereens. Pat, boy, a good woman is… a good woman. 'Tis the first word and the last."

CHAPTER 3

ONCE IN SAN FRANCISCO, Sam Stubener's troubles began. Not that young Pat had a nasty temper, or was grouchy as his father had feared. On the contrary, he was phenomenally sweet and mild. But he was homesick for his beloved mountains. Also, he was secretly appalled by the city, though he trod its roaring streets imperturbable as a red Indian.

"I came down here to fight," he announced, at the end of the first week.

"Where's Jim Hanford?"

Stubener whistled.

"A big champion like him wouldn't look at you," was his answer. "'Go and get a reputation,' is what he'd say."

"I can lick him."

"But the public doesn't know that. If you licked him you'd be champion of the world, and no champion ever became so with his first fight."

"I can."

"But the public doesn't know it, Pat. It wouldn't

come to see you fight. And it's the crowd that brings the money and the big purses. That's why Jim Hanford wouldn't consider you for a second. There'd be nothing in it for him. Besides, he's getting three thousand a week right now in vaudeville, with a contract for twenty-five weeks. Do you think he'd chuck that for a go with a man no one ever heard of? You've got to do something first, make a record. You've got to begin on the little local dubs that nobody ever heard of—guys like Chub Collins, Rough-House Kelly, and the Flying Dutchman. When you've put them away, you're only started on the first round of the ladder. But after that you'll go up like a balloon."

"I'll meet those three named in the same ring one after the other," was Pat's decision. "Make the arrangements accordingly."

Stubener laughed.

"What's wrong? Don't you think I can put them away?"

"I know you can," Stubener assured him. "But it can't be arranged that way. You've got to take them one at a time. Besides, remember, I know the game and I'm managing you. This proposition has to be worked up, and I'm the boy that knows how. If we're lucky, you may get to the top in a couple of years and be the champion with a mint of money."

Pat sighed at the prospect, then brightened up.

"And after that I can retire and go back home to the old man," he said.

Stubener was about to reply, but checked himself. Strange as was this championship material, he felt confident that when the top was reached it would prove very similar to that of all the others who had gone before. Besides, two years was a long way off, and there was much to be done in the meantime.

When Pat fell to moping around his quarters, reading endless poetry books and novels drawn from the public library, Stubener sent him off to live on a Contra Costa ranch across the Bay, under the watchful eye of Spider Walsh. At the end of a week Spider whispered that the job was a cinch. His charge was away and over the hills from dawn till dark, whipping the streams for trout, shooting quail and rabbits, and pursuing the one lone and crafty buck famous for having survived a decade of hunters. It was the Spider who waxed lazy and fat, while his charge kept himself in condition.

As Stubener expected, his unknown was laughed at by the fight club managers. Were not the woods full of unknowns who were always breaking out with championship rashes? A preliminary, say of four rounds—yes, they would grant him that. But the main event—never. Stubener was resolved that young Pat should make his debut in nothing less than a main event, and, by the prestige of his own name he at last managed it. With much misgiving, the Mission Club agreed that Pat Glendon could go fifteen rounds with Rough-House Kelly for a purse of one hundred dollars. It was the custom of young fighters to assume the names of old ring heroes, so no one suspected that he was the son of the great Pat Glendon, while Stubener held his peace. It was a good press surprise package to spring later.

Came the night of the fight, after a month of waiting. Stubener's anxiety was keen. His professional reputation was staked that his man would make a showing, and he was astounded to see Pat, seated in his corner a bare five minutes, lose the healthy color from his cheeks, which turned a sickly yellow.

"Cheer up, boy," Stubener said, slapping him on the shoulder. "The first time in the ring is always strange, and Kelly has a way of letting his opponent wait for him on the chance of getting stage-fright."

"It isn't that," Pat answered. "It's the tobacco smoke. I'm not used to it, and it's making me fair sick."

His manager experienced the quick shock of relief. A man who turned sick from mental causes, even if he were a Samson, could never win to place in the prize ring. As for tobacco smoke, the youngster would have to get used to it, that was all.

Young Pat's entrance into the ring had been met with silence, but when Rough-House Kelly crawled through the ropes his greeting was uproarious. He did not belie his name.

He was a ferocious-looking man, black and hairy, with huge, knotty muscles, weighing a full two hundred pounds. Pat looked across at him curiously, and received a savage scowl. After both had been introduced to the audience, they shook hands. And even as their gloves gripped, Kelly ground his teeth, convulsed his face with an expression of rage, and muttered:

"You've got yer nerve wid yeh." He flung Pat's hand roughly from his, and hissed, "I'll eat yeh up, ye pup!"

The audience laughed at the action, and it guessed hilariously at what Kelly must have said.

Back in his corner, and waiting the gong, Pat turned to Stubener.

"Why is he angry with me?" he asked.

"He ain't," Stubener answered. "That's his way, trying to scare you. It's just mouth-fighting."

"It isn't boxing," was Pat's comment; and Stubener, with a quick glance, noted that his eyes were as mildly blue as ever.

"Be careful," the manager warned, as the gong for the first round sounded and Pat stood up. "He's liable to come at you like a man-eater."

And like a man-eater Kelly did come at him, rushing across the ring in wild fury. Pat, who in his easy way had advanced only a couple of paces, gauged the other's momentum, side-stepped, and brought his stiff-arched right across to the jaw. Then he stood and looked on with a great curiosity. The fight was over. Kelly had fallen like a stricken bullock to the floor, and there he lay without movement while the referee, bending over him, shouted the ten seconds in his unheeding ear. When Kelly's seconds came to lift him, Pat was before them. Gathering the huge, inert bulk of the man in his arms, he carried him to his corner and deposited him on the stool and in the arms of his seconds.

Half a minute later, Kelly's head lifted and his eyes wavered open. He looked about him stupidly and then to one of his seconds.

"What happened?" he queried hoarsely. "Did the roof fall on me?"

CHAPTER 4

AS A RESULT of his fight with Kelly, though the general
opinion was that he had won by a fluke, Pat was matched
with Rufe Mason. This took place three weeks later, and the
Sierra Club audience at Dreamland Rink failed to see what
happened. Rufe Mason was a heavyweight, noted locally for
his cleverness. When the gong for the first round sounded,
both men met in the center of the ring. Neither rushed. Nor
did they strike a blow. They felt around each other, their
arms bent, their gloves so close together that they almost
touched. This lasted for perhaps five seconds. Then it
happened, and so quickly that not one in a hundred of the
audience saw. Rufe Mason made a feint with his right. It was
obviously not a real feint, but a feeler, a mere tentative
threatening of a possible blow. It was at this instant that Pat
loosed his punch. So close together were they that the
distance the blow traveled was a scant eight inches. It was a
short-arm left jolt, and it was accomplished by a twist of the
left forearm and a thrust of the shoulder. It landed flush on
the point of the chin and the astounded audience saw Rufe

Mason's legs crumple under him as his body sank to the floor. But the referee had seen, and he promptly proceeded to count him out. Again Pat carried his opponent to his corner, and it was ten minutes before Rufe Mason, supported by his seconds, with sagging knees and rolling, glassy eyes, was able to move down the aisle through the stupefied and incredulous audience on the way to his dressing room.

"No wonder," he told a reporter, "that Rough-House Kelly thought the roof hit him."

After Chub Collins had been put out in the twelfth second of the first round of a fifteen-round contest, Stubener felt compelled to speak to Pat.

"Do you know what they're calling you now?" he asked.

Pat shook his head.

"One Punch Glendon."

Pat smiled politely. He was little interested in what he was called. He had certain work cut out which he must do ere he could win back to his mountains, and he was phlegmatically doing it, that was all.

"It won't do," his manager continued, with an ominous shake of the head. "You can't go on putting your men out so quickly. You must give them more time."

"I'm here to fight, ain't I?" Pat demanded in surprise.

Again Stubener shook his head.

"It's this way, Pat. You've got to be big and generous in the fighting game. Don't get all the other fighters sore. And it's not fair to the audience. They want a run for their money. Besides, no one will fight you. They'll all be scared out. And you can't draw crowds with ten-second fights. I leave it to you. Would you pay a dollar, or five, to see a ten-second fight?"

Pat was convinced, and he promised to give future audiences the requisite run for their money, though he stated that, personally, he preferred going fishing to witnessing a hundred rounds of fighting.

And still, Pat had got practically nowhere in the game. The local sports laughed when his name was mentioned. It called to mind funny fights and Rough-House Kelly's remark about the roof. Nobody knew how Pat could fight. They had never seen him. Where was his wind, his stamina, his ability to mix it with rough customers through long grueling contests? He had demonstrated nothing but the possession of a lucky punch and a depressing proclivity for flukes.

So it was that his fourth match was arranged with Pete Sosso, a Portuguese fighter from Butchertown, known only for the amazing tricks he played in the ring. Pat did not train for the fight. Instead he made a flying and sorrowful trip to the mountains to bury his father. Old Pat had known well the condition of his heart, and it had stopped suddenly on him.

Young Pat arrived back in San Francisco with so close a margin of time that he changed into his fighting togs directly from his traveling suit, and even then the audience was kept waiting ten minutes.

"Remember, give him a chance," Stubener cautioned him as he climbed through the ropes. "Play with him, but do it seriously. Let him go ten or twelve rounds, then get him."

Pat obeyed instructions, and, though it would have been easy enough to put Sosso out, so tricky was he that to stand up to him and not put him out kept his hands full. It was a pretty exhibition, and the audience was delighted. Sosso's whirlwind attacks, wild feints, retreats, and rushes, required all Pat's science to protect himself, and even then he did not escape unscathed.

Stubener praised him in the minute-rests, and all would have been well, had not Sosso, in the fourth round, played one of his most spectacular tricks. Pat, in a mix-up, had landed a hook to Sosso's jaw, when to his amazement, the latter dropped his hands and reeled backward, eyes rolling, legs bending and giving, in a high state of grogginess. Pat could not understand. It had not been a knock-out blow, and yet there was his man all ready to fall to the mat. Pat dropped his own hands and wonderingly watched his reeling opponent. Sosso staggered away, almost fell, recovered, and staggered obliquely and blindly forward again.

For the first and the last time in his fighting career, Pat was caught off his guard. He actually stepped aside to let the reeling man go by. Still reeling, Sosso suddenly loosed his right. Pat received it full on his jaw with an impact that rattled all his teeth. A great roar of delight went up from the audience. But Pat did not hear. He saw only Sosso before him, grinning and defiant, and not the least bit groggy. Pat was hurt by the blow, but vastly more outraged by the trick. All the wrath that his father ever had surged up in him. He shook his head as if to get rid of the shock of the blow and steadied himself before his man. It all occurred in the next second. With a feint that drew his opponent, Pat fetched his left to the solar plexus, almost at the same instant whipping his right across to the jaw. The latter blow landed on Sosso's mouth ere his falling body struck the floor. The club doctors worked half an hour to bring him to. After that they put eleven stitches in his mouth and packed him off in an ambulance.

"I'm sorry," Pat told his manager, "I'm afraid I lost my temper. I'll never do it again in the ring. Dad always cautioned me about it. He said it had made him lose more than one battle. I didn't know I could lose my temper that way, but now that I know I'll keep it in control."

And Stubener believed him. He was coming to the stage where he could believe anything about his young charge.

"You don't need to get angry," he said, "you're so thoroughly the master of your man at any stage."

"At any inch or second of the fight," Pat affirmed.

"And you can put them out any time you want."

"Sure I can. I don't want to boast. But I just seem to possess the ability. My eyes show me the opening that my skill knows how to make, and time and distance are second nature to me. Dad called it a gift, but I thought he was blarneying me. Now that I've been up against these men, I guess he was right. He said I had the mind and muscle correlation."

"At any inch or second of the fight," Stubener repeated musingly.

Pat nodded, and Stubener, absolutely believing him,

caught a vision of a golden future that should have fetched old Pat out of his grave.

"Well, don't forget, we've got to give the crowd a run for its money," he said. "We'll fix it up between us how many rounds a fight should go. Now your next bout will be with the Flying Dutchman. Suppose you let it run the full fifteen and put him out in the last round. That will give you a chance to make a showing as well."

"All right, Sam," was the answer.

"It will be a test for you," Stubener warned. "You may fail to put him out in that last round."

"Watch me." Pat paused to put weight to his promise, and picked up a volume of Longfellow. "If I don't I'll never read poetry again, and that's going some."

"You bet it is," his manager proclaimed jubilantly, "though what you see in such stuff is beyond me."

Pat sighed, but did not reply. In all his life he had found but one person who cared for poetry, and that had been the red-haired school teacher who scared him off into the woods.

CHAPTER 5

"WHERE ARE YOU GOING?" Stubener demanded in surprise, looking at his watch.

Pat, with his hand on the door-knob, paused and turned around.

"To the Academy of Sciences," he said. "There's a professor who's going to give a lecture there on Browning to-night, and Browning is the sort of writer you need assistance with. Sometimes I think I ought to go to night school."

"But great Scott, man!" exclaimed the horrified manager. "You're on with the Flying Dutchman to-night."

"I know it. But I won't enter the ring a moment before half past nine or quarter to ten. The lecture will be over at nine fifteen. If you want to make sure, come around and pick me up in your machine."

Stubener shrugged his shoulders helplessly.

"You've got no kick coming," Pat assured him. "Dad used to tell me a man's worst time was in the hours just before a fight, and that many a fight was lost by a man's breaking down right there, with nothing to do but think and be anxious. Well, you'll never need to worry about me that way. You ought to be glad I can go off to a lecture."

And later that night, in the course of watching fifteen splendid rounds, Stubener chuckled to himself more than once at the idea of what that audience of sports would think, did it know that this magnificent young prize-fighter had come to the ring directly from a Browning lecture.

The Flying Dutchman was a young Swede who possessed an unwonted willingness to fight and who was blessed with phenomenal endurance. He never rested, was always on the offensive, and rushed and fought from gong to gong. In the out-fighting his arms whirled about like flails, in the in-fighting he was forever shouldering or half-wrestling and starting blows whenever he could get a hand free. From start to finish he was a whirlwind, hence his name. His failing was lack of judgment in time and distance. Nevertheless he had won many fights by virtue of landing one in each dozen or so of the unending fusillades of punches he delivered. Pat, with strong upon him the caution that he must not put his opponent out, was kept busy. Nor, though he escaped vital damage, could he avoid entirely those eternal flying gloves. But it was good training, and in a mild way he enjoyed the contest.

"Could you get him now?" Stubener whispered in his ear during the minute rest at the end of the fifth round.

"Sure," was Pat's answer.

"You know he's never yet been knocked out by any one," Stubener warned a couple of rounds later.

"Then I'm afraid I'll have to break my knuckles," Pat smiled. "I know the punch I've got in me, and when I land it something's got to go. If he won't, my knuckles will."

"Do you think you could get him now?" Stubener asked at the end of the thirteenth round.

"Anytime, I tell you."

"Well, then, Pat, let him run to the fifteenth."

In the fourteenth round the Flying Dutchman exceeded himself. At the stroke of the gong he rushed clear across the ring to the opposite corner where Pat was leisurely getting to his feet. The house cheered, for it knew the Flying Dutchman had cut loose. Pat, catching the fun of it, whimsically decided to meet the terrific onslaught with a wholly passive defense and not to strike a blow. Nor did he strike a blow, nor feint a blow, during the three minutes of whirlwind that followed. He gave a rare exhibition of stalling, sometimes hugging his bowed face with his left arm, his abdomen with his right; at other times, changing as the point of attack changed, so that both gloves were held on either side his face, or both elbows and forearms guarded his mid-section; and all the time moving about, clumsily shouldering, or half-falling forward against his opponent and clogging his efforts; himself never striking nor threatening to strike, the while rocking with the impacts of the storming blows that beat upon his various guards the devil's own tattoo.

Those close at the ringside saw and appreciated, but the rest of the audience, fooled, arose to its feet and roared its applause in the mistaken notion that Pat, helpless, was receiving a terrible beating. With the end of the round, the audience, dumbfounded, sank back into its seats as Pat walked steadily to his corner. It was not understandable. He should have been beaten to a pulp, and yet nothing had happened to him.

"Now are you going to get him?" Stubener queried anxiously.

"Inside ten seconds," was Pat's confident assertion. "Watch me."

There was no trick about it. When the gong struck and Pat bounded to his feet, he advertised it unmistakably that for the first time in the fight he was starting after his man. Not one onlooker misunderstood. The Flying Dutchman read the advertisement, too, and for the first time in his career, as they met in the center of the ring, visibly hesitated. For the fraction of a second they faced each other in position. Then the Flying Dutchman leaped forward upon his man, and Pat, with a timed right-cross, dropped him cold as he leaped.

It was after this battle that Pat Glendon started on his upward rush to fame. The sports and the sporting writers took him up. For the first time the Flying Dutchman had been knocked out. His conqueror had proved a wizard of defense. His previous victories had not been flukes. He had a kick in both his hands. Giant that he was, he would go far. The time was already past, the writers asserted, for him to waste himself on the third-raters and chopping blocks. Where were Ben Menzies, Rege Rede, Bill Tarwater, and Ernest Lawson? It was time for them to meet this young cub that had suddenly shown himself a fighter of quality. Where was his manager anyway, that he was not issuing the challenges?

And then fame came in a day; for Stubener divulged the secret that his man was none other than the son of Pat Glendon, Old Pat, the old-time ring hero. "Young" Pat Glendon, he was promptly christened, and sports and writers flocked about him to admire him, and back him, and write him up.

Beginning with Ben Menzies and finishing with Bill Tarwater, he challenged, fought, and knocked out the four second-raters. To do this, he was compelled to travel, the battles taking place in Goldfield, Denver, Texas, and New York. To accomplish it required months, for the bigger fights were not easily arranged, and the men themselves demanded more time for training.

The second year saw him running to cover and disposing of the half-dozen big fighters that clustered just beneath the top of the heavyweight ladder. On this top, firmly planted, stood "Big" Jim Hanford, the undefeated world champion. Here, on the top rungs, progress was slower, though Stubener was indefatigable in issuing challenges and in promoting sporting opinion to force the man to fight. Will King was disposed of in England, and Glendon pursued Tom Harrison half way around the world to defeat him on Boxing Day in Australia.

But the purses grew larger and larger. In place of a hundred dollars, such as his first battles had earned him, he was now receiving from twenty to thirty thousand dollars a fight, as well as equally large sums from the moving picture men. Stubener took his manager's percentage of all this, according to the terms of the contract old Pat had drawn up, and both he and Glendon, despite their heavy expenses, were waxing rich. This was due, more than anything else, to the clean lives they lived. They were not wasters.

Stubener was attracted to real estate, and his holdings in San Francisco, consisting of building flats and apartment houses, were bigger than Glendon ever dreamed. There was a secret syndicate of bettors, however, which could have made an accurate guess at the size of Stubener's holdings, while heavy bonus after heavy bonus, of which Glendon never heard, was paid over to his manager by the moving picture men.

Stubener's most serious task was in maintaining the innocence of his young gladiator. Nor did he find it difficult. Glendon, who had nothing to do with the business end, was little interested. Besides, wherever his travels took him, he spent his spare time in hunting and fishing. He rarely mingled with those of the sporting world, was notoriously shy and secluded, and preferred art galleries and books of verse to sporting gossip. Also, his trainers and sparring partners were rigorously instructed by the manager to keep their tongues away from the slightest hints of ring rottenness. In every way Stubener intervened between Glendon and the world. He was never even interviewed save in Stubener's presence.

Only once was Glendon approached. It was just prior to his battle with Henderson, and an offer of a hundred thousand was made to him to throw the fight. It was made hurriedly, in swift whispers, in a hotel corridor, and it was fortunate for the man that Pat controlled his temper and shouldered past him without reply. He brought the tale of it to Stubener, who said:

"It's only con, Pat. They were trying to josh you." He noted the blue eyes blaze. "And maybe worse than that. If they could have got you to fall for it, there might have been a big sensation in the papers that would have finished you. But I doubt it. Such things don't happen any more. It's a myth, that's what it is, that has come down from the middle history of the ring. There has been rottenness in the past, but no fighter or manager of reputation would dare anything of the sort to-day. Why, Pat, the men in the game are as clean and straight as those in professional baseball, than which there is nothing cleaner or straighter."

And all the while he talked, Stubener knew in his heart that the forthcoming fight with Henderson was not to be shorter than twelve rounds—this for the moving pictures—and not longer than the fourteenth round. And he knew, furthermore, so big were the stakes involved, that Henderson himself was pledged not to last beyond the fourteenth.

And Glendon, never approached again, dismissed the matter from his mind and went out to spend the afternoon in taking color photographs. The camera had become his latest hobby. Loving pictures, yet unable to paint, he had compromised by taking up photography. In his hand baggage was one grip packed with books on the subject, and he spent long hours in the dark room, realizing for himself the various processes. Never had there been a great fighter who was as aloof from the fighting world as he.

Because he had little to say with those he encountered, he was called sullen and unsocial, and out of this a newspaper reputation took form that was not an exaggeration so much as it was an entire misconception. Boiled down, his character in print was that of an ox-muscled and dumbly stupid brute, and one callow sporting writer dubbed him the "abysmal brute." The name stuck. The rest of the fraternity hailed it with delight, and thereafter Glendon's name never appeared in print unconnected with it. Often, in a headline or under a photograph, "The Abysmal Brute," capitalized and without quotation marks, appeared alone. All the world knew who was this brute. This made him draw into himself closer than ever, while it developed a bitter prejudice against newspaper folk.

Regarding fighting itself, his earlier mild interest grew stronger. The men he now fought were anything but dubs, and victory did not come so easily. They were picked men, experienced ring generals, and each battle was a problem. There were occasions when he found it impossible to put them out in any designated later round of a fight.

Thus, with Sulzberger, the gigantic German, try as he would in the eighteenth round, he failed to get him, in the nineteenth it was the same story, and not till the twentieth did he manage to break through the baffling guard and drop him. Glendon's increasing enjoyment of the game was accompanied by severer and prolonged training. Never dissipating, spending much of his time on hunting trips in the hills, he was practically always in the pink of condition, and, unlike his father, no unfortunate accidents marred his career. He never broke a bone, nor injured so much as a knuckle. One thing that Stubener noted with secret glee was that his young fighter no longer talked of going permanently back to his mountains when he had won the championship away from Jim Hanford.

CHAPTER 6

THE CONSUMMATION of his career was rapidly approaching. The great champion had even publicly intimated his readiness to take on Glendon as soon as the latter had disposed of the three or four aspirants for the championship who intervened. In six months Pat managed to put away Kid McGrath and Philadelphia Jack McBride, and there remained only Nat Powers and Tom Cannam. And all would have been well had not a certain society girl gone adventuring into journalism, and had not Stubener agreed to an interview with the woman reporter of the San Francisco "Courier-Journal."

Her work was always published over the name of Maud Sangster, which, by the way, was her own name. The Sangsters were a notoriously wealthy family. The founder, old Jacob Sangster, had packed his blankets and worked as a farm-hand in the West. He had discovered an inexhaustible borax deposit in Nevada, and, from hauling it out by mule-teams, had built a railroad to do the freighting. Following that, he had poured the profits of borax into the purchase of hundreds and thousands of square miles of timber lands in California, Oregon, and Washington. Still later, he had combined politics with business, bought statesmen, judges, and machines, and become a captain of complicated industry. And after that he had died, full of honor and pessimism, leaving his name a muddy blot for future historians to smudge, and also leaving a matter of a couple of hundreds of millions for his four sons to squabble over. The legal, industrial, and political battles that followed, vexed and amused California for a generation, and culminated in deadly hatred and unspeaking terms between the four sons. The youngest, Theodore, in middle life experienced a change of heart, sold out his stock farms and racing stables, and plunged into a fight with all the corrupt powers of his native state, including most of its millionaires, in a quixotic attempt to purge it of the infamy which had been implanted by old Jacob Sangster.

Maud Sangster was Theodore's oldest daughter. The Sangster stock uniformly bred fighters among the men and beauties among the women. Nor was Maud an exception. Also, she must have inherited some of the virus of adventure from the Sangster breed, for she had come to womanhood and done a multitude of things of which no woman in her position should have been guilty. A match in ten thousand, she remained unmarried. She had sojourned in Europe without bringing home a nobleman for spouse, and had declined a goodly portion of her own set at home. She had gone in for outdoor sports, won the tennis championship of the state, kept the society weeklies agog with her unconventionalities, walked from San Mateo to Santa Cruz against time on a wager, and once caused a sensation by playing polo in a men's team at a private Burlingame practice game. Incidentally, she had gone in for art, and maintained a studio in San Francisco's Latin Quarter.

All this had been of little moment until her father's reform attack became acute. Passionately independent, never yet having met the man to whom she could gladly submit, and bored by those who had aspired, she resented her father's interference with her way of life and put the climax on all her social misdeeds by leaving home and going to work on the "Courier-Journal." Beginning at twenty dollars a week, her salary had swiftly risen to fifty. Her work was principally musical, dramatic, and art criticism, though she was not above mere journalistic stunts if they promised to be sufficiently interesting. Thus she scooped the big interview with Morgan at a time when he was being futilely trailed by a dozen New York star journalists, went down to the bottom of the Golden Gate in a diver's suit, and flew with Rood, the bird man, when he broke all records of continuous flight by reaching as far as Riverside.

Now it must not be imagined that Maud Sangster was a hard-bitten Amazon. On the contrary, she was a gray-eyed, slender young woman, of three or four and twenty, of medium stature, and possessing uncommonly small hands and feet for an outdoor woman or any other kind of a woman. Also, far in excess of most outdoor women, she knew how to be daintily feminine.

It was on her own suggestion that she received the editor's commission to interview Pat Glendon. With the exception of having caught a glimpse, once, of Bob

Fitzsimmons in evening dress at the Palace Grill, she had never seen a prizefighter in her life. Nor was she curious to see one—at least she had not been curious until Young Pat Glendon came to San Francisco to train for his fight with Nat Powers. Then his newspaper reputation had aroused her. The Abysmal Brute!—it certainly must be worth seeing. From what she read of him she gleaned that he was a man-monster, profoundly stupid and with the sullenness and ferocity of a jungle beast. True, his published photographs did not show all that, but they did show the hugeness of brawn that might be expected to go with it. And so, accompanied by a staff photographer, she went out to the training quarters at the Cliff House at the hour appointed by Stubener.

That real estate owner was having trouble. Pat was rebellious. He sat, one big leg dangling over the side of the arm chair and Shakespeare's Sonnets face downward on his knee, orating against the new woman.

"What do they want to come butting into the game for?" he demanded. "It's not their place. What do they know about it anyway? The men are bad enough as it is. I'm not a holy show. This woman's coming here to make me one. I never have stood for women around the training quarters, and I don't care if she is a reporter."

"But she's not an ordinary reporter," Stubener interposed. "You've heard of the Sangsters?—the millionaires?"

Pat nodded.

"Well, she's one of them. She's high society and all that stuff. She could be running with the Blingum crowd now if she wanted to instead of working for wages. Her old man's worth fifty millions if he's worth a cent."

"Then what's she working on a paper for?—keeping some poor devil out of a job."

"She and the old man fell out, had a tiff or something, about the time he started to clean up San Francisco. She quit. That's all—left home and got a job. And let me tell you one thing, Pat: she can everlastingly sling English. There isn't a pen-pusher on the Coast can touch her when she gets going."

Pat began to show interest, and Stubener hurried on.

"She writes poetry, too—the regular la-de-dah stuff, just like you. Only I guess hers is better, because she published a whole book of it once. And she writes up the shows. She interviews every big actor that hits this burg."

"I've seen her name in the papers," Pat commented.

"Sure you have. And you're honored, Pat, by her coming to interview you. It won't bother you any. I'll stick right by and give her most of the dope myself. You know I've always done that."

Pat looked his gratitude.

"And another thing, Pat: don't forget you've got to put up with this interviewing. It's part of your business. It's big advertising, and it comes free. We can't buy it. It interests people, draws the crowds, and it's crowds that pile up the gate receipts." He stopped and listened, then looked at his watch. "I think that's her now. I'll go and get her and bring her in. I'll tip it off to her to cut it short, you know, and it won't take long." He turned in the doorway. "And be decent, Pat. Don't shut up like a clam. Talk a bit to her when she asks you questions."

Pat put the Sonnets on the table, took up a newspaper, and was apparently deep in its contents when the two entered the room and he stood up. The meeting was a mutual shock. When blue eyes met gray, it was almost as if the man and the woman shouted triumphantly to each other, as if each had found something sought and unexpected. But this was for the instant only. Each had anticipated in the other something so totally different that the next moment the clear cry of recognition gave way to confusion. As is the way of women, she was the first to achieve control, and she did it without having given any outward sign that she had ever lost it. She advanced most of the distance across the floor to meet Glendon. As for him, he scarcely knew how he stumbled through the introduction. Here was a woman, a WOMAN. He had not known that such a creature could exist. The few women he had noticed had never prefigured this. He wondered what Old Pat's judgment would have been of her, if she was the sort he had recommended to hang on to with both his hands. He discovered that in some way he was holding her hand. He looked at it, curious and fascinated, marveling at its fragility.

She, on the other hand, had proceeded to obliterate the echoes of that first clear call. It had been a peculiar experience, that was all, this sudden out-rush of her toward this strange man. For was not he the abysmal brute of the prize-ring, the great, fighting, stupid bulk of a male animal who hammered up his fellow males of the same stupid order? She smiled at the way he continued to hold her hand.

"I'll have it back, please, Mr. Glendon," she said. "I... I really need it, you know."

He looked at her blankly, followed her gaze to her imprisoned hand, and dropped it in a rush of awkwardness that sent the blood in a manifest blush to his face.

She noted the blush, and the thought came to her that he did not seem quite the uncouth brute she had pictured. She could not conceive of a brute blushing at anything. And also, she found herself pleased with the fact that he lacked the easy glibness to murmur an apology. But the way he devoured her with his eyes was disconcerting. He stared at her as if in a trance, while his cheeks flushed even more redly.

Stubener by this time had fetched a chair for her, and Glendon automatically sank down into his.

"He's in fine shape, Miss Sangster, in fine shape," the manager was saying. "That's right, isn't it, Pat? Never felt better in your life?"

Glendon was bothered by this. His brows contracted in a troubled way, and he made no reply.

"I've wanted to meet you for a long time, Mr. Glendon," Miss Sangster said. "I never interviewed a pugilist before, so if I don't go about it expertly you'll forgive me, I am sure."

"Maybe you'd better start in by seeing him in action," was the manager's suggestion. "While he's getting into his fighting togs I can tell you a lot about him—fresh stuff, too. We'll call in Walsh, Pat, and go a couple of rounds."

"We'll do nothing of the sort," Glendon growled roughly, in just the way an abysmal brute should. "Go ahead with the interview."

The business went ahead unsatisfactorily. Stubener did most of the talking and suggesting, which was sufficient to irritate Maud Sangster, while Pat volunteered nothing. She studied his fine countenance, the eyes clear blue and wide apart, the well-modeled, almost aquiline, nose, the firm, chaste lips that were sweet in a masculine way in their curl at the corners and that gave no hint of any sullenness. It was a baffling personality, she concluded, if what the papers said of him was so. In vain she sought for earmarks of the brute. And in vain she attempted to establish contacts. For one thing, she knew too little about prize-fighters and the ring, and whenever she opened up a lead it was promptly snatched away by the information-oozing Stubener.

"It must be most interesting, this life of a pugilist," she said once, adding with a sigh, "I wish I knew more about it. Tell me: why do you fight?—Oh, aside from money reasons." (This latter to forestall Stubener). "Do you enjoy fighting? Are you stirred by it, by pitting yourself against other men? I hardly know how to express what I mean, so you must be patient with me."

Pat and Stubener began speaking together, but for once Pat bore his manager down.

"I didn't care for it at first—"

"You see, it was too dead easy for him," Stubener interrupted.

"But later," Pat went on, "when I encountered the better fighters, the real big clever ones, where I was more—"

"On your mettle?" she suggested.

"Yes; that's it, more on my mettle, I found I did care for it... a great deal, in fact. But still, it's not so absorbing to me as it might be. You see, while each battle is a sort of problem which I must work out with my wits and muscle, yet to me the issue is never in doubt—"

"He's never had a fight go to a decision," Stubener proclaimed. "He's won every battle by the knock-out route."

"And it's this certainty of the outcome that robs it of what I imagine must be its finest thrills," Pat concluded.

"Maybe you'll get some of them thrills when you go up against Jim Hanford," said the manager.

Pat smiled, but did not speak.

"Tell me some more," she urged, "more about the way you feel when you are fighting."

And then Pat amazed his manager, Miss Sangster, and himself, by blurting out:

"It seems to me I don't want to talk with you on such things. It's as if there are things more important for you and me to talk about. I—"

He stopped abruptly, aware of what he was saying but unaware of why he was saying it.

"Yes," she cried eagerly. "That's it. That is what makes a good interview—the real personality, you know."

But Pat remained tongue-tied, and Stubener wandered away on a statistical comparison of his champion's weights, measurements, and expansions with those of Sandow, the Terrible Turk, Jeffries, and the other modern strong men. This was of little interest to Maud Sangster, and she showed that she was bored. Her eyes chanced to rest on the Sonnets. She picked the book up and glanced inquiringly at Stubener.

"That's Pat's," he said. "He goes in for that kind of stuff, and color photography, and art exhibits, and such things. But for heaven's sake don't publish anything about it. It would ruin his reputation."

She looked accusingly at Glendon, who immediately became awkward. To her it was delicious. A shy young man, with the body of a giant, who was one of the kings of bruisers, and who read poetry, and went to art exhibits, and experimented with color photography! Of a surety there was no abysmal brute here. His very shyness she divined now was due to sensitiveness and not stupidity. Shakespeare's Sonnets! This was a phase that would bear investigation. But Stubener stole the opportunity away and was back chanting his everlasting statistics.

A few minutes later, and most unwittingly, she opened up the biggest lead of all. That first sharp attraction toward him had begun to stir again after the discovery of the Sonnets. The magnificent frame of his, the handsome face, the chaste lips, the clear-looking eyes, the fine forehead which the short crop of blond hair did not hide, the aura of physical well-being and cleanness which he seemed to emanate—all this, and more that she sensed, drew her as she had never been drawn by any man, and yet through her mind kept running the nasty rumors that she had heard only the day before at the "Courier-Journal" office.

"You were right," she said. "There is something more important to talk about. There is something in my mind I want you to reconcile for me. Do you mind?"

Pat shook his head.

"If I am frank?—abominably frank? I've heard the men, sometimes, talking of particular fights and of the betting odds, and, while I gave no heed to it at the time, it seemed to me it was firmly agreed that there was a great deal of trickery and cheating connected with the sport. Now, when I look at you, for instance, I find it hard to understand how you can be a party to such cheating. I can understand your liking the sport for a sport, as well as for the money it brings you, but I can't understand—"

"There's nothing to understand," Stubener broke in, while Pat's lips were wreathed in a gentle, tolerant smile. "It's all fairy tales, this talk about faking, about fixed fights, and all that rot. There's nothing to it, Miss Sangster, I assure you. And now let me tell you about how I discovered Mr. Glendon. It was a letter I got from his father—"

But Maud Sangster refused to be side-tracked, and addressed herself to Pat.

"Listen. I remember one case particularly. It was some fight that took place several months ago—I forget the contestants. One of the editors of the "Courier-Journal" told me he intended to make a good winning. He didn't hope; he said he intended. He said he was on the inside and was betting on the number of rounds. He told me the fight would end in the nineteenth. This was the night before. And the next day he triumphantly called my attention to the fact that it had ended in that very round. I didn't think anything of it one way or the other. I was not interested in prize-fighting then. But I am now. At the time it seemed quite in accord with the vague conception I had about fighting. So you see, it isn't all fairy tales, is it?"

"I know that fight," Glendon said. "It was Owen and Murgweather. And it did end in the nineteenth round, Sam. And she said she heard that round named the day before. How do you account for it, Sam?"

"How do you account for a man picking a lucky lottery ticket?" the manager evaded, while getting his wits together to answer. "That's the very point. Men who study form and condition and seconds and rules and such things often pick the number of rounds, just as men have been known to pick hundred-to-one shots in the races. And don't forget one thing: for every man that wins, there's another that loses, there's another that didn't pick right. Miss Sangster, I assure you, on my honor, that faking and fixing in the fight game is... is non-existent."

"What is your opinion, Mr. Glendon?" she asked.

"The same as mine," Stubener snatched the answer. "He knows what I say is true, every word of it. He's never fought anything but a straight fight in his life. Isn't that right, Pat?"

"Yes; it's right," Pat affirmed, and the peculiar thing to Maud Sangster was that she was convinced he spoke the truth.

She brushed her forehead with her hand, as if to rid herself of the bepuzzlement that clouded her brain.

"Listen," she said. "Last night the same editor told me that your forthcoming fight was arranged to the very round in which it would end."

Stubener was verging on a panic, but Pat's speech saved him from replying.

"Then the editor lies," Pat's voice boomed now for the first time.

"He did not lie before, about that other fight," she challenged.

"What round did he say my fight with Nat Powers would end in?"

Before she could answer, the manager was into the thick of it.

"Oh, rats, Pat!" he cried. "Shut up. It's only the regular run of ring rumors. Let's get on with this interview."

He was ignored by Glendon, whose eyes, bent on hers, were no longer mildly blue, but harsh and imperative. She was sure now that she had stumbled on something tremendous, something that would explain all that had baffled her. At the same time she thrilled to the mastery of his voice and gaze. Here was a male man who would take hold of life and shake out of it what he wanted.

"What round did the editor say?" Glendon reiterated his demand.

"For the love of Mike, Pat, stop this foolishness," Stubener broke in.

"I wish you would give me a chance to answer," Maud Sangster said.

"I guess I'm able to talk with Miss Sangster," Glendon added. "You get out, Sam. Go off and take care of that photographer."

They looked at each other for a tense, silent moment, then the manager moved slowly to the door, opened it, and turned his head to listen.

"And now what round did he say?"

"I hope I haven't made a mistake," she said tremulously, "but I am very sure that he said the sixteenth round."

She saw surprise and anger leap into Glendon's face, and the anger and accusation in the glance he cast at his manager, and she knew the blow had driven home.

And there was reason for his anger. He knew he had talked it over with Stubener, and they had reached a decision to give the audience a good run for its money without unnecessarily prolonging the fight, and to end it in the sixteenth. And here was a woman, from a newspaper office, naming the very round.

Stubener, in the doorway, looked limp and pale, and it was evident he was holding himself together by an effort.

"I'll see you later," Pat told him. "Shut the door behind you."

The door closed, and the two were left alone. Glendon did not speak. The expression on his face was frankly one of trouble and perplexity.

"Well?" she asked.

He got up and towered above her, then sat down again, moistening his lips with his tongue.

"I'll tell you one thing," he finally said "The fight won't end in the sixteenth round."

She did not speak, but her unconvinced and quizzical smile hurt him.

"You wait and see, Miss Sangster, and you'll see that editor man is mistaken."

"You mean the program is to be changed?" she queried audaciously.

He quivered to the cut of her words.

"I am not accustomed to lying," he said stiffly, "even to women."

"Neither have you to me, nor have you denied the program is to be changed. Perhaps, Mr. Glendon, I am stupid, but I fail to see the difference in what number the final round occurs so long as it is predetermined and known."

"I'll tell you that round, and not another soul shall know."

She shrugged her shoulders and smiled.

"It sounds to me very much like a racing tip. They are always given that way, you know. Furthermore, I am not quite stupid, and I know there is something wrong here. Why were you made angry by my naming the round? Why were you angry with your manager? Why did you send him from the room?"

For reply, Glendon walked over to the window, as if to look out, where he changed his mind and partly turned, and she knew, without seeing, that he was studying her face. He came back and sat down.

"You've said I haven't lied to you, Miss Sangster, and you were right. I haven't." He paused, groping painfully for a correct statement of the situation. "Now do you think you can believe what I am going to tell you? Will you take the word of a... prize-fighter?"

She nodded gravely, looking him straight in the eyes and certain that what he was about to tell was the truth.

"I've always fought straight and square. I've never touched a piece of dirty money in my life, nor attempted a dirty trick. Now I can go on from that. You've shaken me up pretty badly by what you told me. I don't know what to make of it. I can't pass a snap judgment on it. I don't know. But it looks bad. That's what troubles me. For see you, Stubener and I have talked this fight over, and it was understood between us that I would end the fight in the sixteenth round. Now you bring the same word. How did that editor know? Not from me. Stubener must have let it out… unless…" He stopped to debate the problem. "Unless that editor is a lucky guesser. I can't make up my mind about it. I'll have to keep my eyes open and wait and learn. Every word I've given you is straight, and there's my hand on it."

Again he towered out of his chair and over to her. Her small hand was gripped in his big one as she arose to meet him, and after a fair, straight look into the eyes between them, both glanced unconsciously at the clasped hands. She felt that she had never been more aware that she was a woman. The sex emphasis of those two hands—the soft and fragile feminine and the heavy, muscular masculine—was startling. Glendon was the first to speak.

"You could be hurt so easily," he said; and at the same time she felt the firmness of his grip almost caressingly relax.

She remembered the old Prussian king's love for giants, and laughed at the incongruity of the thought-association as she withdrew her hand.

"I am glad you came here to-day," he said, then hurried on awkwardly to make an explanation which the warm light of admiration in his eyes belied. "I mean because maybe you have opened my eyes to the crooked dealing that has been going on."

"You have surprised me," she urged. "It seemed to me that it is so generally understood that prize-fighting is full of crookedness, that I cannot understand how you, one of its chief exponents, could be ignorant of it. I thought as a matter of course that you would know all about it, and now you have convinced me that you never dreamed of it. You must be different from other fighters."

He nodded his head.

"That explains it, I guess. And that's what comes of keeping away from it—from the other fighters, and promoters, and sports. It was easy to pull the wool over my eyes. Yet it remains to be seen whether it has really been pulled over or not. You see, I am going to find out for myself."

"And change it?" she queried, rather breathlessly, convinced somehow that he could do anything he set out to accomplish.

"No; quit it," was his answer. "If it isn't straight I won't have anything more to do with it. And one thing is certain: this coming fight with Nat Powers won't end in the sixteenth round. If there is any truth in that editor's tip, they'll all be fooled. Instead of putting him out in the sixteenth, I'll let the fight run on into the twenties. You wait and see."

"And I'm not to tell the editor?"

She was on her feet now, preparing to go.

"Certainly not. If he is only guessing, let him take his chances. And if there's anything rotten about it he deserves to lose all he bets. This is to be a little secret between you and me. I'll tell you what I'll do. I'll name the round to you. I won't run it into the twenties. I'll stop Nat Powers in the eighteenth."

"And I'll not whisper it," she assured him.

"I'd like to ask you a favor," he said tentatively. "Maybe it's a big favor."

She showed her acquiescence in her face, as if it were already granted, and he went on:

"Of course, I know you won't use this faking in the interview. But I want more than that. I don't want you to publish anything at all."

She gave him a quick look with her searching gray eyes, then surprised herself by her answer.

"Certainly," she said. "It will not be published. I won't write a line of it."

"I knew it," he said simply.

For the moment she was disappointed by the lack of thanks, and the next moment she was glad that he had not thanked her. She sensed the different foundation he was building under this meeting of an hour with her, and she became daringly explorative.

"How did you know it?" she asked.

"I don't know." He shook his head. "I can't explain it. I knew it as a matter of course. Somehow it seems to me I know a lot about you and me."

"But why not publish the interview? As your manager says, it is good advertising."

"I know it," he answered slowly. "But I don't want to know you that way. I think it would hurt if you should publish it. I don't want to think that I knew you professionally. I'd like to remember our talk here as a talk between a man and a woman. I don't know whether you understand what I'm driving at. But it's the way I feel. I want to remember this just as a man and a woman."

As he spoke, in his eyes was all the expression with which a man looks at a woman. She felt the force and beat of him, and she felt strangely tongue-tied and awkward before this man who had been reputed tongue-tied and awkward. He could certainly talk straighter to the point and more convincingly than most men, and what struck her most forcibly was her own inborn certainty that it was mere naïve and simple frankness on his part and not a practised artfulness.

He saw her into her machine, and gave her another thrill when he said good-by. Once again their hands were clasped as he said:

"Some day I'll see you again. I want to see you again. Somehow I have a feeling that the last word has not been said between us."

And as the machine rolled away she was aware of a similar feeling. She had not seen the last of this very disquieting Pat Glendon, king of the bruisers and abysmal brute.

Back in the training quarters, Glendon encountered his perturbed manager.

"What did you fire me out for?" Stubener demanded. "We're finished. A hell of a mess you've made. You've never stood for meeting a reporter alone before, and now you'll see when that interview comes out."

Glendon, who had been regarding him with cool

amusement, made as if to turn and pass on, and then changed his mind.

"It won't come out," he said.

Stubener looked up sharply.

"I asked her not to," Glendon explained.

Then Stubener exploded.

"As if she'd kill a juicy thing like that."

Glendon became very cold and his voice was harsh and grating.

"It won't be published. She told me so. And to doubt it is to call her a liar."

The Irish flame was in his eyes, and by that, and by the unconscious clenching of his passion-wrought hands, Stubener, who knew the strength of them, and of the man he faced, no longer dared to doubt.

Chapter 7

IT DID NOT take Stubener long to find out that Glendon intended extending the distance of the fight, though try as he would he could get no hint of the number of the round. He wasted no time, however, and privily clinched certain arrangements with Nat Powers and Nat Powers' manager. Powers had a faithful following of bettors, and the betting syndicate was not to be denied its harvest.

On the night of the fight, Maud Sangster was guilty of a more daring unconventionality than any she had yet committed, though no whisper of it leaked out to shock society. Under the protection of the editor, she occupied a ring-side seat. Her hair and most of her face were hidden under a slouch hat, while she wore a man's long overcoat that fell to her heels. Entering in the thick of the crowd, she was not noticed; nor did the newspaper men, in the press seats against the ring directly in front of her, recognize her.

As was the growing custom, there were no preliminary bouts, and she had barely gained her seat when roars of applause announced the arrival of Nat Powers. He came down the aisle in the midst of his seconds, and she was almost frightened by the formidable bulk of him. Yet he leaped the ropes as lightly as a man half his weight, and grinned acknowledgment to the tumultuous greeting that arose from all the house. He was not pretty. Two cauliflower ears attested his profession and its attendant brutality, while his broken nose had been so often spread over his face as to defy the surgeon's art to reconstruct it.

Another uproar heralded the arrival of Glendon, and she watched him eagerly as he went through the ropes to his corner. But it was not until the tedious time of announcements, introductions, and challenges was over, that the two men threw off their wraps and faced each other in ring costume. Concentrated upon them from overhead was the white glare of many electric lights—this for the benefit of the moving picture cameras; and she felt, as she looked at the two sharply contrasted men, that it was in Glendon that she saw the thoroughbred and in Powers the abysmal brute. Both looked their parts—Glendon, clean cut in face and form, softly and massively beautiful, Powers almost asymmetrically rugged and heavily matted with hair.

As they made their preliminary pose for the cameras, confronting each other in fighting attitudes, it chanced that Glendon's gaze dropped down through the ropes and rested on her face. Though he gave no sign, she knew, with a swift leap of the heart, that he had recognized her. The next moment the gong sounded, the announcer cried "Let her go!" and the battle was on.

It was a good fight. There was no blood, no marring, and both were clever. Half of the first round was spent in feeling each other out, but Maud Sangster found the play and feint and tap of the gloves sufficiently exciting. During some of the fiercer rallies in later stages of the fight, the editor was compelled to touch her arm to remind her who she was and where she was.

Powers fought easily and cleanly, as became the hero of half a hundred ring battles, and an admiring claque applauded his every cleverness. Yet he did not unduly exert himself save in occasional strenuous rallies that brought the audience yelling to its feet in the mistaken notion that he was getting his man.

It was at such a moment, when her unpractised eye could not inform her that Glendon was escaping serious damage, that the editor leaned to her and said:

"Young Pat will win all right. He's a comer, and they can't stop him. But he'll win in the sixteenth and not before."

"Or after?" she asked.

She almost laughed at the certitude of her companion's negative. She knew better.

Powers was noted for hunting his man from moment to moment and round to round, and Glendon was content to accede to this program. His defense was admirable, and he threw in just enough of offense to whet the edge of the audience's interest. Though he knew he was scheduled to lose, Powers had had too long a ring experience to hesitate from knocking his man out if the opportunity offered. He had had the double cross worked too often on him to be chary in working it on others. If he got his chance he was prepared to knock his man out and let the syndicate go hang. Thanks to clever press publicity, the idea was prevalent that at last Young Glendon had met his master. In his heart, Powers, however, knew that it was himself who had encountered the better man. More than once, in the faster in-fighting, he received the weight of punches that he knew had been deliberately made no heavier.

On Glendon's part, there were times and times when a slip or error of judgment could have exposed him to one of his antagonist's sledge-hammer blows and lost him the fight. Yet his was that almost miraculous power of accurate timing and distancing, and his confidence was not shaken by the several close shaves he experienced. He had never lost a fight, never been knocked down, and he had always been so thoroughly the master of the man he faced, that such a possibility was unthinkable.

At the end of the fifteenth round, both men were in good condition, though Powers was breathing a trifle heavily and there were men in the ringside seats offering odds that he would "blow up."

It was just before the gong for the sixteenth round struck that Stubener, leaning over Glendon from behind in his corner, whispered:

"Are you going to get him now?"

Glendon, with a back toss of his head, shook it and laughed mockingly up into his manager's anxious face.

With the stroke of the gong for the sixteenth round, Glendon was surprised to see Powers cut loose. From the first second it was a tornado of fighting, and Glendon was hard put to escape serious damage. He blocked, clinched, ducked, sidestepped, was rushed backward against the ropes and was met by fresh rushes when he surged out to center. Several times Powers left inviting openings, but Glendon refused to loose the lightning-bolt of a blow that would drop his man. He was reserving that blow for two rounds later. Not in the whole fight had he ever exerted his full strength, nor struck with the force that was in him.

For two minutes, without the slightest let-up, Powers went at him hammer and tongs. In another minute the round would be over and the betting syndicatehard hit. But that minute was not to be. They had just come together in the center of the ring. It was as ordinary a clinch as any in the fight, save that Powers was struggling and roughing it every instant. Glendon whipped his left over in a crisp but easy jolt to the side of the face. It was like any of a score of similar jolts he had already delivered in the course of the fight. To his amazement he felt Powers go limp in his arms and begin sinking to the floor on sagging, spraddling legs that refused to bear his weight. He struck the floor with a thump, rolled half over on his side, and lay with closed eyes and motionless. The referee, bending above him, was shouting the count.

At the cry of "Nine!" Powers quivered as if making a vain effort to rise.

"Ten!—and out!" cried the referee.

He caught Glendon's hand and raised it aloft to the roaring audience in token that he was the winner.

For the first time in the ring, Glendon was dazed. It had not been a knockout blow. He could stake his life on that. It had not been to the jaw but to the side of the face, and he knew it had gone there and nowhere else. Yet the man was out, had been counted out, and he had faked it beautifully. That final thump on the floor had been a convincing masterpiece. To the audience it was indubitably a knockout, and the moving picture machines would perpetuate the lie. The editor had called the turn after all, and a crooked turn it was.

Glendon shot a swift glance through the ropes to the face of Maud Sangster. She was looking straight at him, but her eyes were bleak and hard, and there was neither recognition nor expression in them. Even as he looked, she turned away unconcernedly and said something to the man beside her.

Powers' seconds were carrying him to his corner, a seeming limp wreck of a man. Glendon's seconds were advancing upon him to congratulate him and to remove his gloves. But Stubener was ahead of them. His face was beaming as he caught Glendon's right glove in both his hands and cried:

"Good boy, Pat. I knew you'd do it."

Glendon pulled his glove away. And for the first time in the years they had been together, his manager heard him swear.

"You go to hell," he said, and turned to hold out his hands for his seconds to pull off the gloves.

CHAPTER 8

THAT NIGHT, after receiving the editor's final dictum that there was not a square fighter in the game, Maud Sangster cried quietly for a moment on the edge of her bed, grew angry, and went to sleep hugely disgusted with herself, prize-fighters, and the world in general.

The next afternoon she began work on an interview with Henry Addison that was destined never to be finished. It was in the private room that was accorded her at the "Courier-Journal" office that the thing happened. She had paused in her writing to glance at a headline in the afternoon paper announcing that Glendon was matched with Tom Cannam, when one of the door-boys brought in a card. It was Glendon's.

"Tell him I can't be seen," she told the boy.

In a minute he was back.

"He says he's coming in anyway, but he'd rather have your permission."

"Did you tell him I was busy?" she asked.

"Yes'm, but he said he was coming just the same."

She made no answer, and the boy, his eyes shining with admiration for the importunate visitor, rattled on.

"I know'm. He's a awful big guy. If he started roughhousing he could clean the whole office out. He's young Glendon, who won the fight last night."

"Very well, then. Bring him in. We don't want the office cleaned out, you know."

No greetings were exchanged when Glendon entered. She was as cold and inhospitable as a gray day, and neither invited him to a chair nor recognized him with her eyes, sitting half turned away from him at her desk and waiting for him to state his business. He gave no sign of how this cavalier treatment affected him, but plunged directly into his subject.

"I want to talk to you," he said shortly. "That fight. It did end in that round."

She shrugged her shoulders.

"I knew it would."

"You didn't," he retorted. "You didn't. I didn't."

She turned and looked at him with quiet affectation of boredom.

"What is the use?" she asked. "Prize-fighting is prize-fighting, and we all know what it means. The fight did end in the round I told you it would."

"It did," he agreed. "But you didn't know it would. In all the world you and I were at least two that knew Powers wouldn't be knocked out in the sixteenth."

She remained silent.

"I say you knew he wouldn't." He spoke peremptorily, and, when she still declined to speak, stepped nearer to her. "Answer me," he commanded.

She nodded her head.

"But he was," she insisted.

"He wasn't. He wasn't knocked out at all. Do you get that? I am going to tell you about it, and you are going to listen. I didn't lie to you. Do you get that? I didn't lie to you. I was a fool, and they fooled me, and you along with me. You thought you saw him knocked out. Yet the blow I struck was not heavy enough. It didn't hit him in the right place either. He made believe it did. He faked that knockout."

He paused and looked at her expectantly. And somehow, with a leap and thrill, she knew that she believed him, and she felt pervaded by a warm happiness at the reinstatement of this man who meant nothing to her and whom she had seen but twice in her life.

"Well?" he demanded, and she thrilled anew at the compellingness of him.

She stood up, and her hand went out to his.

"I believe you," she said. "And I am glad, most glad."

It was a longer grip than she had anticipated. He looked at her with eyes that burned and to which her own unconsciously answered back. Never was there such a man, was her thought. Her eyes dropped first, and his followed, so that, as before, both gazed at the clasped hands. He made a movement of his whole body toward her, impulsive and involuntary, as if to gather her to him, then checked himself abruptly, with an unmistakable effort. She saw it, and felt the pull of his hand as it started to draw her to him. And to her amazement she felt the desire to yield, the desire almost overwhelmingly to be drawn into the strong circle of those arms. And had he compelled, she knew that she would not have refrained. She was almost dizzy, when he checked himself and with a closing of his fingers that half crushed hers, dropped her hand, almost flung it from him.

"God!" he breathed. "You were made for me."

He turned partly away from her, sweeping his hand to his forehead. She knew she would hate him forever if he dared one stammered word of apology or explanation. But he seemed to have the way always of doing the right thing where she was concerned. She sank into her chair, and he into another, first drawing it around so as to face her across the corner of the desk.

"I spent last night in a Turkish bath," he said. "I sent for an old broken-down bruiser. He was a friend of my father in the old days. I knew there couldn't be a thing about the ring he didn't know, and I made him talk. The funny thing was that it was all I could do to convince him that I didn't know the things I asked him about. He called me the babe in the woods. I guess he was right. I was raised in the woods, and woods is about all I know.

"Well, I received an education from that old man last night. The ring is rottener than you told me. It seems everybody connected with it is crooked. The very supervisors that grant the fight permits graft off of the promoters; and the promoters, managers, and fighters graft off of each other and off the public. It's down to a system, in one way, and on the other hand they're always—do you know what the double cross is?" (She nodded.) "Well, they don't seem to miss a chance to give each other the double cross.

"The stuff that old man told me took my breath away. And here I've been in the thick of it for several years and knew nothing of it. I was a real babe in the woods. And yet I can see how I've been fooled. I was so made that nobody could stop me. I was bound to win, and, thanks to Stubener, everything crooked was kept away from me. This morning I cornered Spider Walsh and made him talk. He was my first trainer, you know, and he followed Stubener's instructions. They kept me in ignorance. Besides, I didn't herd with the sporting crowd. I spent my time hunting and fishing and monkeying with cameras and such things. Do you know what Walsh and Stubener called me between themselves?—the Virgin. I only learned it this morning from Walsh, and it was like pulling teeth. And they were right. I was a little innocent lamb.

"And Stubener was using me for crookedness, too, only I didn't know it. I can look back now and see how it was worked. But you see, I wasn't interested enough in the game to be suspicious. I was born with a good body and a cool head, I was raised in the open, and I was taught by my father, who knew more about fighting than any man living or dead. It was too easy. The ring didn't absorb me. There was never any doubt of the outcome. But I'm done with it now."

She pointed to the headline announcing his match with Tom Cannam.

"That's Stubener's work," he explained. "It was programmed months ago. But I don't care. I'm heading for the mountains. I've quit."

She glanced at the unfinished interview on the desk

and sighed.

"How lordly men are," she said. "Masters of destiny. They do as they please—"

"From what I've heard," he interrupted, "you've done pretty much as you please. It's one of the things I like about you. And what has struck me hard from the first was the way you and I understand each other."

He broke off and looked at her with burning eyes.

"Well, the ring did one thing for me," he went on. "It made me acquainted with you. And when you find the one woman, there's just one thing to do. Take her in your two hands and don't let go. Come on, let us start for the mountains."

It had come with the suddenness of a thunder-clap, and yet she felt that she had been expecting it. Her heart was beating up and almost choking her in a strangely delicious way. Here at least was the primitive and the simple with a vengeance. Then, too, it seemed a dream. Such things did not take place in modern newspaper offices. Love could not be made in such fashion; it only so occurred on the stage and in novels.

He had arisen, and was holding out both hands to her.

"I don't dare," she said in a whisper, half to herself. "I don't dare."

And thereat she was stung by the quick contempt that flashed in his eyes but that swiftly changed to open incredulity.

"You'd dare anything you wanted," he was saying. "I know that. It's not a case of dare, but of want. Do you want?"

She had arisen, and was now swaying as if in a dream. It flashed into her mind to wonder if it were hypnotism. She wanted to glance about her at the familiar objects of the room in order to identify herself with reality, but she could not take her eyes from his. Nor did she speak.

He had stepped beside her. His hand was on her arm, and she leaned toward him involuntarily. It was all part of the dream, and it was no longer hers to question anything. It was the great dare. He was right. She could dare what she wanted, and she did want. He was helping her into her jacket. She was thrusting the hat-pins through her hair. And even as she realized it, she found herself walking beside him through the opened door. The "Flight of the Duchess" and "The Statue and the Bust," darted through her mind. Then she remembered "Waring."

"'What's become of Waring?'" she murmured.

"'Land travel or sea-faring?'" he murmured back.

And to her this kindred sufficient note was a vindication of her madness.

At the entrance of the building he raised his hand to call a taxi, but was stopped by her touch on his arm.

"Where are we going?" she breathed.

"To the Ferry. We've just time to catch that Sacramento train."

"But I can't go this way," she protested. "I... I haven't even a change of handkerchiefs."

He held up his hand again before replying.

"You can shop in Sacramento. We'll get married there and catch the night overland north. I'll arrange everything by telegraph from the train."

As the cab drew to the curb, she looked quickly about her at the familiar street and the familiar throng, then, with almost a flurry of alarm, into Glendon's face.

"I don't know a thing about you," she said.

"We know everything about each other," was his answer.

She felt the support and urge of his arms, and lifted her foot to the step. The next moment the door had closed, he was beside her, and the cab was heading down Market Street. He passed his arm around her, drew her close, and kissed her. When next she glimpsed his face she was certain that it was dyed with a faint blush.

"I... I've heard there was an art in kissing," he stammered. "I don't know anything about it myself, but I'll learn. You see, you're the first woman I ever kissed."

CHAPTER 9

WHERE A JAGGED PEAK of rock thrust above the vast virgin forest, reclined a man and a woman. Beneath them, on the edge of the trees, were tethered two horses. Behind each saddle were a pair of small saddle-bags. The trees were monotonously huge. Towering hundreds of feet into the air, they ran from eight to ten and twelve feet in diameter. Many were much larger. All morning they had toiled up the divide through this unbroken forest, and this peak of rock had been the first spot where they could get out of the forest in order to see the forest.

Beneath them and away, far as they could see, lay range upon range of haze-empurpled mountains. There was no end to these ranges. They rose one behind another to the dim, distant skyline, where they faded away with a vague promise of unending extension beyond. There were no clearings in the forest; north, south, east, and west, untouched, unbroken, it covered the land with its mighty growth.

They lay, feasting their eyes on the sight, her hand

clasped in one of his; for this was their honeymoon, and these were the redwoods of Mendocino. Across from Shasta they had come, with horses and saddle-bags, and down through the wilds of the coast counties, and they had no plan except to continue until some other plan entered their heads. They were roughly dressed, she in travel-stained khaki, he in overalls and woolen shirt. The latter was open at the sunburned neck, and in his hugeness he seemed a fit dweller among the forest giants, while for her, as a dweller with him, there were no signs of aught else but happiness.

"Well, Big Man," she said, propping herself up on an elbow to gaze at him, "it is more wonderful than you promised. And we are going through it together."

"And there's a lot of the rest of the world we'll go through together," he answered, shifting his position so as to get her hand in both of his.

"But not till we've finished with this," she urged. "I seem never to grow tired of the big woods... and of you."

He slid effortlessly into a sitting posture and gathered her into his arms.

"Oh, you lover," she whispered. "And I had given up hope of finding such a one."

"And I never hoped at all. I must just have known all the time that I was going to find you. Glad?"

Her answer was a soft pressure where her hand rested on his neck, and for long minutes they looked out over the great woods and dreamed.

"You remember I told you how I ran away from the red-haired school teacher? That was the first time I saw this country. I was on foot, but forty or fifty miles a day was play for me. I was a regular Indian. I wasn't thinking about you then. Game was pretty scarce in the redwoods, but there was plenty of fine trout. That was when I camped on these rocks. I didn't dream that some day I'd be back with you, YOU."

"And be a champion of the ring, too," she suggested.

"No; I didn't think about that at all. Dad had always told me I was going to be, and I took it for granted. You see, he was very wise. He was a great man."

"But he didn't see you leaving the ring."

"I don't know. He was so careful in hiding its crookedness from me, that I think he feared it. I've told you about the contract with Stubener. Dad put in that clause about crookedness. The first crooked thing my manager did was to break the contract."

"And yet you are going to fight this Tom Cannam. Is it worth while?"

He looked at her quickly.

"Don't you want me to?"

"Dear lover, I want you to do whatever you want."

So she said, and to herself, her words still ringing in her ears, she marveled that she, not least among the stubbornly independent of the breed of Sangster, should utter them. Yet she knew they were true, and she was glad.

"It will be fun," he said.

"But I don't understand all the gleeful details."

"I haven't worked them out yet. You might help me. In the first place I'm going to double-cross Stubener and the betting syndicate. It will be part of the joke. I am going to put Cannam out in the first round. For the first time I shall be really angry when I fight. Poor Tom Cannam, who's as crooked as the rest, will be the chief sacrifice. You see, I intend to make a speech in the ring. It's unusual, but it will be a success, for I am going to tell the audience all the inside workings of the game. It's a good game, too, but they're running it on business principles, and that's what spoils it. But there, I'm giving the speech to you instead of at the ring."

"I wish I could be there to hear," she said.

He looked at her and debated.

"I'd like to have you. But it's sure to be a rough time. There is no telling what may happen when I start my program. But I'll come straight to you as soon as it's over. And it will be the last appearance of Young Glendon in the ring, in any ring."

"But, dear, you've never made a speech in your life," she objected. "You might fail."

He shook his head positively.

"I'm Irish," he announced, "and what Irishman was there who couldn't speak?" He paused to laugh merrily. "Stubener thinks I'm crazy. Says a man can't train on matrimony. A lot he knows about matrimony, or me, or you, or anything except real estate and fixed fights. But I'll show him that night, and poor Tom, too. I really feel sorry for Tom."

"My dear abysmal brute is going to behave most abysmally and brutally, I fear," she murmured.

He laughed.

"I'm going to make a noble attempt at it. Positively my last appearance, you know. And then it will be you, YOU. But if you don't want that last appearance, say the word."

"Of course I want it, Big Man. I want my Big Man for himself, and to be himself he must be himself. If you want this, I want it for you, and for myself, too. Suppose I said I wanted to go on the stage, or to the South Seas or the North Pole?"

He answered slowly, almost solemnly.

"Then I'd say go ahead. Because you are you and must be yourself and do whatever you want. I love you because you are you."

"And we're both a silly pair of lovers," she said, when his embrace had relaxed.

"Isn't it great!" he cried.

He stood up, measured the sun with his eye, and extended his hand out over the big woods that covered the serried, purple ranges.

"We've got to sleep out there somewhere. It's thirty miles to the nearest camp."

CHAPTER 10

WHO, OF ALL the sports present, will ever forget the memorable night at the Golden Gate Arena, when Young Glendon put Tom Cannam to sleep and an even greater one than Tom Cannam, kept the great audience on the ragged edge of riot for an hour, caused the subsequent graft investigation of the supervisors and the indictments of the contractors and the building commissioners, and pretty generally disrupted the whole fight game. It was a complete surprise. Not even Stubener had the slightest apprehension of what was coming. It was true that his man had been insubordinate after the Nat Powers affair, and had run off and got married; but all that was over. Young Pat had done the expected, swallowed the inevitable crookedness of the ring, and come back into it again.

The Golden Gate Arena was new. This was its first fight, and it was the biggest building of the kind San Francisco had ever erected. It seated twenty-five thousand, and every seat was occupied. Sports had traveled from all the world to be present, and they had paid fifty dollars for their ring-side seats. The cheapest seat in the house had sold for five dollars.

The old familiar roar of applause went up when Billy Morgan, the veteran announcer, climbed through the ropes and bared his gray head. As he opened his mouth to speak, a heavy crash came from a near section where several tiers of low seats had collapsed. The crowd broke into loud laughter and shouted jocular regrets and advice to the victims, none of whom had been hurt. The crash of the seats and the hilarious uproar caused the captain of police in charge to look at one of his lieutenants and lift his brows in token that they would have their hands full and a lively night.

One by one, welcomed by uproarious applause, seven doughty old ring heroes climbed through the ropes to be introduced. They were all ex-heavy-weight champions of the world. Billy Morgan accompanied each presentation to the audience with an appropriate phrase. One was hailed as "Honest John" and "Old Reliable," another was "the squarest two-fisted fighter the ring ever saw." And of others: "the hero of a hundred battles and never threw one and never lay down"; "the gamest of the old guard"; "the only one who ever came back"; "the greatest warrior of them all"; and "the hardest nut in the ring to crack."

All this took time. A speech was insisted on from each of them, and they mumbled and muttered in reply with proud blushes and awkward shamblings. The longest speech was from "Old Reliable" and lasted nearly a minute. Then they had to be photographed. The ring filled up with celebrities, with champion wrestlers, famous conditioners, and veteran time-keepers and referees. Light-weights and middle-weights swarmed. Everybody seemed to be challenging everybody. Nat Powers was there, demanding a return match from Young Glendon, and so were all the other shining lights whom Glendon had snuffed out. Also, they all challenged Jim Hanford, who, in turn, had to make his statement, which was to the effect that he would accord the next fight to the winner of the one that was about to take place. The audience immediately proceeded to name the winner, half of it wildly crying "Glendon," and the other half "Powers." In the midst of the pandemonium another tier of seats went down, and half a dozen rows were on between cheated ticket holders and the stewards who had been reaping a fat harvest. The captain despatched a message to headquarters for additional police details.

The crowd was feeling good. When Cannam and Glendon made their ring entrances the Arena resembled a national political convention. Each was cheered for a solid five minutes. The ring was now cleared. Glendon sat in his corner surrounded by his seconds. As usual, Stubener was at his back. Cannam was introduced first, and after he had scraped and ducked his head, he was compelled to respond to the cries for a speech. He stammered and halted, but managed to grind out several ideas.

"I'm proud to be here to-night," he said, and found space to capture another thought while the applause was thundering. "I've fought square. I've fought square all my life. Nobody can deny that. And I'm going to do my best to-night."

There were loud cries of: "That's right, Tom!" "We

know that!" "Good boy, Tom!" "You're the boy to fetch the bacon home!"

Then came Glendon's turn. From him, likewise, a speech was demanded, though for principals to give speeches was an unprecedented thing in the prize-ring. Billy Morgan held up his hand for silence, and in a clear, powerful voice Glendon began.

"Everybody has told you they were proud to be here to-night," he said. "I am not" The audience was startled, and he paused long enough to let it sink home, "I am not proud of my company. You wanted a speech. I'll give you a real one. This is my last fight. After to-night I leave the ring for good. Why? I have already told you. I don't like my company. The prize-ring is so crooked that no man engaged in it can hide behind a corkscrew. It is rotten to the core, from the little professional clubs right up to this affair to-night."

The low rumble of astonishment that had been rising at this point burst into a roar. There were loud boos and hisses, and many began crying: "Go on with the fight!" "We want the fight!" "Why don't you fight?" Glendon, waiting, noted that the principal disturbers near the ring were promoters and managers and fighters. In vain did he strive to make himself heard. The audience was divided, half crying out, "Fight!" and the other half, "Speech! Speech!"

Ten minutes of hopeless madness prevailed. Stubener, the referee, the owner of the Arena, and the promoter of the fight, pleaded with Glendon to go on with the fight. When he refused, the referee declared that he would award the fight in forfeit to Cannam if Glendon did not fight.

"You can't do it," the latter retorted. "I'll sue you in all the courts if you try that on, and I'll not promise you that you'll survive this crowd if you cheat it out of the fight. Besides, I'm going to fight. But before I do I'm going to finish my speech."

"But it's against the rules," protested the referee.

"It's nothing of the sort. There's not a word in the rules against ring-side speeches. Every big fighter here to-night has made a speech."

"Only a few words," shouted the promoter in Glendon's ear. "But you're giving a lecture."

"There's nothing in the rules against lectures," Glendon answered. "And now you fellows get out of the ring or I'll throw you out."

The promoter, apoplectic and struggling, was dropped over the ropes by his coat-collar. He was a large man, but so easily had Glendon done it with one hand that the audience went wild with delight. The cries for a speech increased in volume. Stubener and the owner beat a wise retreat. Glendon held up his hands to be heard, whereupon those that shouted for the fight redoubled their efforts. Two or three tiers of seats crashed down, and numbers who had thus lost their places, added to the turmoil by making a concerted rush to squeeze in on the still intact seats, while those behind, blocked from sight of the ring, yelled and raved for them to sit down.

Glendon walked to the ropes and spoke to the police captain. He was compelled to bend over and shout in his ear.

"If I don't give this speech," he said, "this crowd will wreck the place. If they break loose you can never hold them, you know that. Now you've got to help. You keep the ring clear and I'll silence the crowd."

He went back to the center of the ring and again held up his hands.

"You want that speech?" he shouted in a tremendous voice.

Hundreds near the ring heard him and cried "Yes!"

"Then let every man who wants to hear shut up the noise-maker next to him!"

The advice was taken, so that when he repeated it, his voice penetrated farther. Again and again he shouted it, and slowly, zone by zone, the silence pressed outward from the ring, accompanied by a muffled undertone of smacks and thuds and scuffles as the obstreperous were subdued by their neighbors. Almost had all confusion been smothered, when a tier of seats near the ring went down. This was greeted with fresh roars of laughter, which of itself died away, so that a lone voice, far back, was heard distinctly as it piped: "Go on, Glendon! We're with you!"

Glendon had the Celt's intuitive knowledge of the psychology of the crowd. He knew that what had been a vast disorderly mob five minutes before was now tightly in hand, and for added effect he deliberately delayed. Yet the delay was just long enough and not a second too long. For thirty seconds the silence was complete, and the effect produced was one of awe. Then, just as the first faint hints of restlessness came to his ears, he began to speak:

"When I finish this speech," he said, "I am going to fight. I promise you it will be a real fight, one of the few real fights you have ever seen. I am going to get my man in the shortest possible time. Billy Morgan, in making his final announcement, will tell you that it is to be a forty-five-round contest. Let me tell you that it will be nearer forty-five seconds.

"When I was interrupted I was telling you that the ring was rotten. It is—from top to bottom. It is run on business principles, and you all know what business principles are. Enough said. You are the suckers, every last one of you that is not making anything out of it. Why are the seats falling down to-night? Graft. Like the fight game, they were built on business principles."

He now held the audience stronger than ever, and knew it.

"There are three men squeezed on two seats. I can see that everywhere. What does it mean? Graft. The stewards don't get any wages. They are supposed to graft. Business principles again. You pay. Of course you pay. How are the fight permits obtained? Graft. And now let me ask you: if the men who build the seats graft, if the stewards graft, if the authorities graft, why shouldn't those higher up in the fight game graft? They do. And you pay.

"And let me tell you it is not the fault of the fighters. They don't run the game. The promoters and managers run it; they're the business men. The fighters are only fighters. They begin honestly enough, but the managers and promoters make them give in or kick them out. There have been straight fighters. And there are now a few, but they don't earn much as a rule. I guess there have been straight managers. Mine is about the best of the boiling. But just ask him how much he's got salted down in real estate and apartment houses.”

Here the uproar began to drown his voice.

“Let every man who wants to hear shut up the man alongside of him!” Glendon instructed.

Again, like the murmur of a surf, there was a rustling of smacks, and thuds, and scuffles, and the house quieted down.

“Why does every fighter work overtime insisting that he’s always fought square? Why are they called Honest Johns, and Honest Bills, and Honest Blacksmiths, and all the rest? Doesn’t it ever strike you that they seem to be afraid of something? When a man comes to you shouting he is honest, you get suspicious. But when a prize-fighter passes the same dope out to you, you swallow it down.

“May the best man win! How often have you heard Billy Morgan say that! Let me tell you that the best man doesn’t win so often, and when he does it’s usually arranged for him. Most of the grudge fights you’ve heard or seen were arranged, too. It’s a program. The whole thing is programmed. Do you think the promoters and managers are in it for their health? They’re not. They’re business men.

“Tom, Dick, and Harry are three fighters. Dick is the best man. In two fights he could prove it. But what happens? Tom licks Harry. Dick licks Tom. Harry licks Dick. Nothing proved. Then come the return matches. Harry licks Tom. Tom licks Dick. Dick licks Harry. Nothing proved. Then they try again. Dick is kicking. Says he wants to get along in the game. So Dick licks Tom, and Dick licks Harry. Eight fights to prove Dick the best man, when two could have done it. All arranged. A regular program. And you pay for it, and when your seats don't break down you get robbed of them by the stewards.

"It's a good game, too, if it were only square. The fighters would be square if they had a chance. But the graft is too big. When a handful of men can divide up three-quarters of a million dollars on three fights—"

A wild outburst compelled him to stop. Out of the medley of cries from all over the house, he could distinguish such as "What million dollars?" "What three fights?" "Tell us!" "Go on!" Likewise there were boos and hisses, and cries of "Muckraker! Muckraker!"

"Do you want to hear?" Glendon shouted. "Then keep order!"

Once more he compelled the impressive half minute of silence.

"What is Jim Hanford planning? What is the program his crowd and mine are framing up? They know I've got him. He knows I've got him. I can whip him in one fight. But he's the champion of the world. If I don't give in to the program, they'll never give me a chance to fight him. The program calls for three fights. I am to win the first fight. It will be pulled off in Nevada if San Francisco won't stand for it. We are to make it a good fight. To make it good, each of us will put up a side bet of twenty thousand. It will be real money, but it won't be a real bet. Each gets his own slipped back to him. The same way with the purse. We'll divide it evenly, though the public division will be thirty-five and sixty-five. The purse, the moving picture royalties, the advertisements, and all the rest of the drags won't be a cent less than two hundred and fifty thousand. We'll divide it, and go to work on the return match. Hanford will win that, and we divide again. Then comes the third fight; I win as I have every right to; and we have taken three-quarters of a million out of the pockets of the fighting public. That's the program, but the money is dirty. And that's why I am quitting the ring to-night—"

It was at this moment that Jim Hanford, kicking a clinging policeman back among the seat-holders, heaved his huge frame through the ropes, bellowing: "It's a lie!"

He rushed like an infuriated bull at Glendon, who sprang back, and then, instead of meeting the rush, ducked cleanly away. Unable to check himself, the big man fetched up against the ropes. Flung back by the spring of them, he was turning to make another rush, when Glendon landed him. Glendon, cool, clear-seeing, distanced his man perfectly to the jaw and struck the first full-strength blow of his career. All his strength, and his reserve of strength, went into that one smashing muscular explosion.

Hanford was dead in the air—in so far as unconsciousness may resemble death. So far as he was concerned, he ceased at the moment of contact with Glendon's fist. His feet left the floor and he was in the air until he struck the topmost rope. His inert body sprawled across it, sagged at the middle, and fell through the ropes and down out of the ring upon the heads of the men in the press seats.

The audience broke loose. It had already seen more than it had paid to see, for the great Jim Hanford, the world champion, had been knocked out. It was unofficial, but it had been with a single punch. Never had there been such a night in fistiana. Glendon looked ruefully at his damaged knuckles, cast a glance through the ropes to where Hanford was groggily coming to, and held up his hands. He had clinched his right to be heard, and the audience grew still.

"When I began to fight," he said, "they called me 'One-Punch Glendon.' You saw that punch a moment ago. I always had that punch. I went after my men and got them on the jump, though I was careful not to hit with all my might. Then I was educated. My manager told me it wasn't fair to the crowd. He advised me to make long fights so that the crowd could get a run for its money. I was a fool, a mutt. I was a green lad from the mountains. So help me God, I swallowed it as the truth. My manager used to talk over with me what round I would put my man out in. Then he tipped it off to the betting syndicate, and the betting syndicate went to it. Of course you paid. But I am glad for one thing. I never touched a cent of the money. They didn't dare offer it to me, because they knew it would give the game away.

"You remember my fight with Nat Powers. I never knocked him out. I had got suspicious. So the gang framed it up with him. I didn't know. I intended to let him go a couple of rounds over the sixteenth. That last punch in the sixteenth didn't shake him. But he faked the knock-out just the same and fooled all of you."

"How about to-night?" a voice called out. "Is it a frame-up?"

"It is," was Glendon's answer. "How's the syndicate betting? That Cannam will last to the fourteenth."

Howls and hoots went up. For the last time Glendon held up his hand for silence.

"I'm almost done now. But I want to tell you one thing. The syndicate gets landed to-night. This is to be a square fight. Tom Cannam won't last till the fourteenth round. He won't last the first round."

Cannam sprang to his feet in his corner and cried out in a fury:

"You can't do it. The man don't live who can get me in one round!"

Glendon ignored him and went on.

"Once now in my life I have struck with all my strength. You saw that a moment ago when I caught Hanford. To-night, for the second time, I am going to hit with all my strength—that is, if Cannam doesn't jump through the ropes right now and get away. And now I'm ready."

He went to his corner and held out his hands for his gloves. In the opposite corner Cannam raged while his seconds tried vainly to calm him. At last Billy Morgan managed to make the final announcement.

"This will be a forty-five round contest," he shouted. "Marquis of Queensbury Rules! And may the best man win! Let her go!"

The gong struck. The two men advanced. Glendon's right hand was extended for the customary shake, but Cannam, with an angry toss of the head, refused to take it. To the general surprise, he did not rush. Angry though he was, he fought carefully, his touched pride impelling him to bend every effort to last out the round. Several times he struck, but he struck cautiously, never relaxing his defense. Glendon hunted him about the ring, ever advancing with the remorseless tap-tap of his left foot. Yet he struck no blows, nor attempted to strike. He even dropped his hands to his sides and hunted the other defenselessly in an effort to draw him out. Cannam grinned defiantly, but declined to take advantage of the proffered opening.

Two minutes passed, and then a change came over Glendon. By every muscle, by every line of his face, he advertised that the moment had come for him to get his man. Acting it was, and it was well acted. He seemed to have become a thing of steel, as hard and pitiless as steel. The effect was apparent on Cannam, who redoubled his caution. Glendon quickly worked him into a corner and herded and held him there. Still he struck no blow, nor attempted to strike, and the suspense on Cannam's part grew painful. In vain he tried to work out of the corner, while he could not summon resolution to rush upon his opponent in an attempt to gain the respite of a clinch.

Then it came—a swift series of simple feints that were muscle flashes. Cannam was dazzled. So was the audience. No two of the onlookers could agree afterward as to what took place. Cannam ducked one feint and at the same time threw up his face guard to meet another feint for his jaw. He also attempted to change position with his legs. Ring-side witnesses swore that they saw Glendon start the blow from his right hip and leap forward like a tiger to add the weight of his body to it. Be that as it may, the blow caught Cannam on the point of the chin at the moment of his shift of position. And like Hanford, he was unconscious in the air before he struck the ropes and fell through on the heads of the reporters.

Of what happened afterward that night in the Golden Gate Arena, columns in the newspapers were unable adequately to describe. The police kept the ring clear, but they could not save the Arena. It was not a riot. It was an orgy. Not a seat was left standing. All over the great hall, by main strength, crowding and jostling to lay hands on beams and boards, the crowd uprooted and over-turned. Prize-fighters sought protection of the police, but there were not enough police to escort them out, and fighters, managers, and promoters were beaten and battered. Jim Hanford alone was spared. His jaw, prodigiously swollen, earned him this mercy. Outside, when finally driven from the building, the crowd fell upon a new seven-thousand-dollar motor car belonging to a well-known fight promoter and reduced it to scrapiron and kindling wood.

Glendon, unable to dress amid the wreckage of dressing rooms, gained his automobile, still in his ring costume and wrapped in a bath robe, but failed to escape. By weight of numbers the crowd caught and held his machine. The police were too busy to rescue him, and in the end a compromise was effected, whereby the car was permitted to proceed at a walk escorted by five thousand cheering madmen.

It was midnight when this storm swept past Union Square and down upon the St. Francis. Cries for a speech went up, and though at the hotel entrance, Glendon was good-naturedly restrained from escaping. He even tried leaping out upon the heads of the enthusiasts, but his feet never touched the pavement. On heads and shoulders, clutched at and uplifted by every hand that could touch his body, he went back through the air to the machine. Then he gave his speech, and Maud Glendon, looking down from an upper window at her young Hercules towering on the seat of the automobile, knew, as she always knew, that he meant it when he repeated that he had fought his last fight and retired from the ring forever.

THE END

www.ingramcontent.com/pod-product-compliance
Lightning Source LLC
Chambersburg PA
CBHW030737110726

47900CB00008B/2337